A Place Called Hope

A Story About Living the Thoughts of God

A Place Called Hope

A Story About Living the Thoughts of God

James John Ross

Dowit Press

Paperback: ISBN:978-0-615-99726-1

Printed in The United States of America.

□■ A BUYER'S INTRODUCTION ■□

The idea for this story was sold to me by God.

There was no burning bush. No chiseled etchings on a stone tablet. No parting of the seas, or a booming voice from the heavens above. Early one morning, He simply knelt down beside me and whispered in my ear an offer that I couldn't refuse.

I understand the notion of Almighty God attempting to sell anything to anyone, might be hard for some to believe-perhaps even a bit blasphemous to others. Still it happens to all of us, each and every day; we're just not aware that it's God who does the selling. Call Him what you will: The Almighty, the Muse, an Angel, the Divine Spirit, Zelda the Good Witch or plain old positive thinking. Whatever name you choose, it is essentially the source of creation attempting to make a sale.

I can use His product, that's why I bought this idea.

Why He sold it to me I do not know. I was merely sold the story-asked to write it, and share it with you. I cannot take credit for the impact of its message, or the value of its teachings. I was asked to purchase the idea and serve it as a vessel; I agreed. I had to conceptualize the idea. That's what people do. We put things in context to help us make sense of the surreal. Though I was given a dash of poetic license, I am for the most part a humble scribe.

The principles you are about to read are as old as mankind. They are ubiquitous in nature, in us and all around us. You can find them on virtually any bookshelf, magazine rack, or dentists' waiting room table in the world. These concepts are not a legend, nor are they folklore, a myth, a ghost story or campfire tale. They are real. As real as the book you are now holding in your hands. I hope their impact on you will be as immeasurable and as life altering as they have been for me. All of us have been sold on these concepts and principles in a variety of ways, ideas which entice us to move forward in life, for the betterment of ourselves, and for those around us.

While it is true the events of the following story have yet to take place, I have no doubt that someday they could in fact happen. Why? As I mentioned, the idea was sold to me by God, and I trust His word (at least it says I should on all my money. And if you can't trust your money, what can you trust?)

I told you the idea for this story was sold to me by God. This is true. He has offered to sell me a few of His products, over the years, but I wasn't buying, until now...

Now when God offers the goods, I am willing to pay the price...no questions asked. And I hope you will be convinced too, as well.

◻◼ PROLOGUE ◼◻

The year is 2257. After nearly a half century of plague, famine, and war, the population of the world has been reduced to less than a half billion souls.

From the ashes of this chaos rose the malevolent Company imposing its dominance over the worlds' remaining war-weary and beleaguered survivors. This evil Company controls virtually all the world's resources, including its most precious asset, the thoughts of man. (The seeds of this conflict are currently germinating in the mind of every person on earth today.)

Only a few scores of holdouts remain, continuing their battle for the right to choose their thoughts freely. They settle on a wooded stretch of land, near the sea, in a place they call Hope.

However, most survivors have settled into a life of misery and servitude under Company rule. The technology and progress of mankind has ceased to exist. Man has essentially regressed back into a Stone Age existence.

Decades after the conflict, into this bleak existence is born Uriah, a boy who chooses to question Company law by refusing to purchase the thoughts forced upon him. This is his story.

"I want to know God's thoughts, the rest are details."
Albert Einstein

"I love to think of nature as an unlimited broadcasting station, through which God speaks to us every hour, if we will only tune in."-George Washington Carver

"We shall steer safely through every storm, so long as our heart is right, our intention fervent, our courage steadfast, and our trust fixed on God."-St. Francis De Sales

"Man finds it hard to get what he wants because he does not want the best. God finds it hard to give because He would give the best and man will not take it."-George MacDonald

"I can see how it might be possible for a man to look down upon the earth and be an atheist, but I cannot conceive how he could look up into the heavens and say there is no God."-Abraham Lincoln

□■ ONE ■□

For the first time in his life, Uriah was alone with his thoughts.

Although he preferred the social interaction of community living—his friends, his grandfather and of course, his beloved Akuna, he had not been willing to surrender his thoughts any longer.

Yet, it was this community, his hometown of Kwo owned by the Company, which had cast him out into a dangerous and unforgiving world. He had been banished into the wilderness, essentially a death sentence for anyone unfortunate enough to receive such a harsh judgment.

He had been driven from Kwo in the traditional manner, at the tip of a spear. He was paraded through the rubble-filled streets and past the caved-in dwellings of the town center. He was marched past the graffiti lined walls he saw day-after-day on his way to work, and as he passed, he read the messages, "feel the hate," "be greed," and "god is nowhere," for the final time. The citizens, people who had been his friends and neighbors only days before, lined the streets on either side hurling garbage or waste at him as he lowered his head in shame. Refuse was always readily available on the unkempt streets of Kwo. The authorities saw to it that all who refused to purchase the thoughts of the Company were given this same humiliating sendoff. Uriah and his shame, would serve as an example to others who might consider buying their thoughts elsewhere.

Once outside the city walls, Uriah watched as the sentry labored to pull the thirty –foot-high thick, wooden gates behind him. They slammed shut with a resounding thud. To Uriah, the sound echoed with finality and isolation. In his lifetime, he had never ventured outside these walls. In that moment, he felt completely alone in the world. He turned to walk when a voice from the guard tower, on top of the wall, called out to him.

"Hey boy, let's see your thoughts keep you alive out there," laughed the guard, as he pointed to the vast expanse of nothingness outside of Kwo.

Uriah said nothing. He began to walk toward the open plain, but inside something beckoned him to look back toward the foreboding stone wall, walls which had served as his home since the day he was born.

"Do not turn around," he told himself. "Keep walking." But after only a few more steps, the urge to look back became too great and Uriah turned. On the wall to his left, he could see his grandfather; his look was one of deep sadness. His face had contorted into a twisted grimace, as if fighting to hold back his tears. Next to his grandfather stood Akuna. Uriah looked up to her and saw tears run down her face. They locked eyes for a few seconds, and then she turned and ran, disappearing from his view. For the first time in his life, no longer subject to the laws of the Company, Uriah was able to feel a deep love toward his grandfather and Akuna, yet he feared it might be the last time he would see either of them again.

Uriah could not bear to look any longer. He turned to face the emptiness of space before him. The heaviness within his heart was almost too much for him to carry. He took a few steps and then began to bawl, uncontrollably.

He did not turn back, again, until Kwo was miles behind him.

□■ TWO ■□

Uriah was barely twenty years old but appeared much younger. He was slender and malnourished, as were all residents of Kwo. His worn blue jeans and soiled tee shirt hung loosely from his waist and shoulders. A knotted length of twine was secured around the beltline of his pants to keep them from falling to his ankles.

His hair was an unkempt, dirty brown, which he constantly brushed from his face revealing a pair of soft, light blue eyes. Those who knew him said they held a childlike gaze. To criminals and conmen, he appeared an easy mark for anyone who might seek a quick score. Yet behind those childlike eyes bore an inner strength, more powerful than they appeared. Uriah knew he would need every ounce of that strength to combat the isolation and the dangers he would face.

He had managed to survive nearly three weeks, being especially careful to avoid any vicious animals that might be lurking about. Packs of wild dogs were known to roam the lands in search of an easy meal. More importantly, he was cautious of the even more dangerous two-legged predators that would kill him, for even his most meager belongings.

He remembered well the stories his grandfather had told him—those stories of bandits, robbers, and wanderers of the wild with the most malicious of intent, and particularly those stories of the roving bands of cannibals, which preyed upon unwary travelers. For Uriah, living in the town of Kwo under Company rule was tantamount to slavery. Yet, there was a level of safety and protection within the walled community.

Unlike Uriah, most citizens believed it was better to be alive and enslaved than be free and dead. In Kwo, the Company sold them misery, but for most, it was a misery they were used to living with. He felt an icy chill run down the center of his back with these thoughts. He quickly steered his attention toward pleasant things, such as the stories of his grandfather and the quiet moments spent alone.

His thoughts also often drifted to Akuna. They had grown up together as friends and neighbors, but in his heart Uriah, had always felt more. He knew he loved her from the first moment seeing her; and though thoughts of love were outlawed in Kwo, he believed she also loved him. He often visualized the deepness of her brown eyes, the soft lilting tone of her voice, and the crescent shaped birthmark on her neck, which had not faded with time. He wondered if she had missed him or if they would ever see one another again. Although thoughts of Akuna would bring him joy, he found they distracted him, in this wilderness and he needed to be alert, he knew thinking of her could get him killed.

Uriah understood he was more fortunate than many who had been excommunicated from their communities. For several weeks leading up to his expulsion from Kwo, he had sensed they would turn him out into the wild. Armed with this internal knowledge, he was able to set aside a few bits of food each day, from his daily allotment, storing it away in anticipation of his release. It was difficult at first; the amount of food allowed by the Company was paltry, at best, and barely enough to sustain a young man with a growing appetite. But now he was incredibly thankful for the inspiration and will power to do so. Water was another matter entirely, as it was always in short supply in Kwo. But heavy rain just days before his expulsion allowed Uriah to capture all the water he could carry.

In spite of this foresight, after just over a week in the wild, even with careful rationing, his food supply had diminished considerably. A small quarter loaf of grain bread, a handful of synthetic raisins, and barely a cup of water were all that remained. It would last one, or maybe two days more, if he rationed carefully. When it was gone, he knew the madness of hunger would come quickly; and he and the beasts, which roamed the wild, would undoubtedly leap closer to one another along the evolutionary scale.

In addition to his stash of food, he was sent out with his journal; a scratched and tarnished wristwatch, a rusted pocketknife, a piece of thick pine (he had fashioned into a walking stick), an unpolished Larimar stone which he kept strictly for its aesthetic value, a change of clothes, and a bedroll with his backpack.

Uriah happened across several small towns, dotted along the vast, barren landscape. Although these towns were not walled and heavily guarded like Kwo, he quickly learned that they too fell under Company rule. He entered these places carefully. On few occasions, he was able to trade spare articles of his clothing with local residents in exchange for food or water. One day, he had grown so hungry that he traded for a dried and rotten, barely edible piece of fruit in return for the Larimar gem stone he had in his possession. Uriah had kept the stone carefully hidden, since he found it, as a child. He knew the Company would have confiscated it if discovered, as they did all possessions of beauty and comfort. The stone was a beautiful keepsake that Uriah prized greatly, but he made a sacrifice to stay alive.

Since Uriah did not have much with which to barter, once he had run out of tangible items to trade, he would rely primarily upon human compassion. To residents in all the towns under the control of the Company, his method was a dangerous proposition. Compassion, like all emotions and thoughts not offered by the Company, was strictly forbidden. Nearly all of these townspeople turned him away.

This left the only possession he had remaining: an array of stories which his grandfather had passed on to him. He had lost both his parents as a young boy, each succumbing to the misery and hardship of life, in Kwo, within weeks of one another. In danger of becoming another Company-owned orphan, he was taken in by his grandfather. His grandfather told him stories of ideas, inspirations, and thoughts offered by God. It was these stories Uriah sought to share, in return for food and water. But even these ideas, the towns' inhabitants had refused to hear for fear of persecution. Uriah realized there had been many towns owned and operated by the same Company that owned Kwo. Just as in Kwo, these stories Uriah offered were outlawed. Many residents threatened to deliver him to the Company, if he didn't leave their town immediately. On one occasion, he narrowly escaped arrest when one of the residents had told the authorities about his offer to sell a competing idea. The penalties handed down for violations of these laws, were similar as to those in Kwo: arrest, expulsion, torture, and in some cases, execution.

With each successive town Uriah entered, he knew the Company would keep a close watch on him, as they did with all outsiders. Within moments of his arrival to a new community, the Company's leaders quickly determined he was a nonconformist, one who would refuse to adhere to their ideals and principles. The result was usually the same, "consume our product or leave immediately." Uriah would soon be sent on his way back into the wild.

In spite of these reactions, he secretly remained grateful for any kindness he received from the townspeople. He felt the fear and misery of each, knowing the few who helped him had risked much. Uriah knew he would not last much longer in the wild, yet the thought of remaining in one of these towns and assimilating was, in his mind, a greater tragedy than venturing back into the unknown countryside. In his heart, he believed he was a willing a participant to leave these places, as he was driven from them; and this was a truth which Uriah could live with.

Besides, there was a place he sought—a town that his grandfather had told him of in secret whispers, late at night, when all other townspeople had turned in for the night. His grandfather told him of a place by the sea, one of enlightenment and imagination, a town where people were free to choose those thoughts and ideas which served them. A town where goals were pursued and dreams fulfilled. A place where happiness and love were a choice of each individual, and each had the freedom to obtain these thoughts. He told Uriah there was a place where the thoughts of God were sold, and Uriah often wondered: how he could be nostalgic for those things he had never before experienced. But in his heart, he knew he belonged in this place.

Yet Uriah wasn't certain if this place existed, at least not the way which his grandfather had described it, and he had not met anyone who had been there to confirm these tales.

He had told Uriah many stories over the years, stories of magical healers and men with minds of a genius. He told him of flying machines which circled the sky above, and ships of steel that could cover the earths' oceans. He told him of small handheld machines that people used to speak to one another from great distances and of boxes with pictures and sounds that transported images from across the globe, including even the heavens. And he told him the earth was once a place where man was free to choose his thoughts and each had the freedom to express these thoughts, but that the Great War had sent man and his ways back to his beginnings. Back to a time before the great accomplishments of man, back to an age of survival and subsequent Company rule.

Even as a young boy, Uriah found many of these stories hard to believe. But something inside of him sensed that his grandfather's story of this magical place, where the thoughts of God were available, must be true. Perhaps it was the sparkle in the old man's eyes when he spoke of this place. Perhaps it was because, even as a young boy, Uriah knew the consequences his grandfather faced, for telling stories about such a place. Would he risk being imprisoned, tortured, or worse in order to amuse a small child with a bedtime story? No, he thought, such a place existed. Uriah knew it just as he could feel it tug at his heart, calling him to "come." His grandfather's stories had to be true, and such a place must still exist. Uriah's life depended upon it.

Uriah knew that the Company had heard the rumblings and gossip of their customers, men with thoughts like his grandfather, and they did not welcome the competition. Yet, rather than convincing their buyers this mystical town did not exist, they merely sold its residents on the rumor that it was a place of evil fraught with danger, disease, and certain death to all who ventured within its borders. They claimed it had become a place where flesh eating hordes now roamed the streets, and any unsuspecting soul foolish enough to enter this place would never return.

It was an easy enough story to sell. After all, fear and deception were two of the Company's best selling products.

If it was true that the unforgiving lands outside of Kwo had been left to the desperate scavengers, and the rabid, starving cannibals, then it was also quite probable this magical town had been overwhelmed by enough of these heartless barbarians, that it had been turned into a sanctuary for evil doers. Yet something inside Uriah's heart pressed him to continue toward this place.

His grandfather's stories had been vague about its location, saying only that it lay on the shores of the sea, beneath the brightest star in the sky.

Uriah had been heading west toward the star since leaving Kwo. He could hear his grandfather's voice in his head, "...beneath the brightest star along the shore."

He traveled mostly in the last few hours of the day and the first several hours after nightfall in order to avoid detection by thieves and murderers. He also consumed much less water after dark. He could hear the howling of animals and the rustling of bushes on some nights, but he caught only shadows of the perpetrators. He suspected they were waiting for him, to slow and weaken, before making their attack.

In spite of his desire to reach the land he sought, Uriah knew the animals wouldn't have much longer to wait, and for this he was oddly grateful. With dusk setting upon him, he had grown too exhausted to continue. He had walked barely a mile, a sign he was growing increasingly weaker.

He searched for a safe place to sleep, finding two bushes at the crest of a ridge. They were small, about two feet high, and the branches were sparse, offering little cover for concealment, however twenty yards away and slightly down the hill stood two large oak trees, set a few feet apart. Sleeping under the trees would leave Uriah exposed, but the artistry of leaves fell perfectly over the ground, providing an adequate shadow from the moon's lamp. It was not the safest of quarters, but he was at least concealed among the shadows from any preying eyes.

Uriah laid his bedroll and blanket on the hard, unforgiving ground and flopped down on top of them. The ground beneath him was covered with small earthen mounds and jagged egg-sized rocks, but he was exhausted and too numb to care. His feet had swollen considerably, stretching the fabric of his moccasins to their tearing point. His barren stomach growled loudly; he feared it might draw attention from any attackers. He was far too tired to put up much of a resistance, if discovered.

Uriah held a last biscuit-sized piece of bread and a dozen or so dried-synthetic raisins, which he had gotten from a woman in the last town he had visited. He had drunk the remains of his water a few hours earlier and now regretted this decision. His parched throat made it uncomfortable to swallow, and he decided he would not make the same mistake with his meager supply of food. He had become an excellent manager at rationing his food store and would need the small amount of energy to continue his search. As hungry as he was, if he were to eat now, he would wake up starving and empty with nothing to combat the hunger. He would save his food for breakfast, hoping it would not be his last.

Uriah was nearly unconscious before his head touched the ground. He would sleep soundly tonight; the crying howls of animals or footsteps nearby would serve as the background music in his dreams. A moment before he closed his eyes Uriah thought he saw a small speck of rotating light in the distance. It appeared and then disappeared several times. "A star perhaps," he thought. "It must be a st-," but he was too tired to open his eyes again, too tired to think.

With the faint smell of salt air in his nose, Uriah fell into a deep, uninterrupted slumber.

☐■ THREE ■☐

Uriah awoke the next morning. He rose gradually, as if emerging from a comatose state; he took a few moments to gather his bearings. His neck had stiffened overnight from the hard ground, but he couldn't remember when he had slept so soundly. It was one of the benefits of complete exhaustion he figured. Uriah rubbed his belly trying to soothe the expanding emptiness. He was glad he had saved his last bits of food until now.

He removed the last of his food from his backpack and tore off a corner of the bread. He bowed his head, giving thanks for these last crumbs of bread. This act was also outlawed in Kwo. Uriah looked around to make certain no one was watching him while he did this. It was a habit he had developed, after a lifetime under Company rule.

Uriah placed the bread in his mouth and chewed, attempting to wash it down with the juice of several of the hybrid raisins. To his disappointment, the raisins had staled and become as dry as the bread. In spite of this, he savored each bite knowing it could be his last meal. He took another bite of the bread and a few more of the raisins. His throat was more parched than before, but at least he was gaining some energy from the food. He would need water soon, very soon.

"Something last night..." he thought, while he ate. Uriah tried to shake the cobwebs of sleep from his head. He looked out over the horizon, during the night a heavy fog had settled over the valley floor below. Uriah had developed a habit of thinking of the day ahead, yet this morning his thoughts were about the evening before. An unformed picture danced in his head. Something had occurred before he slept? Fragmented memories of a dream perhaps? What was it? Stars…, shining…, lights? Unnatural lights?

"The light," he shouted!

Uriah quickly gulped down the last bit of food and stood up between the two large oaks, cinching the rope around his waist a little tighter. He peered down into the fog below but his eyes had yet to catch up to his body. He tried to focus, but could see only the heavy mist.

Suddenly sections of the mist began to clear. Tears in the blanket of milky fog began to form, revealing fragmented holes, of dark blue covered with specks of white. Simultaneously, the fog in his head also began to lift as if the two were somehow inexorably linked. The holes in the fog stretched wider, and for first time in his life Uriah could see the blue of the ocean water. Even through his limited scope, it was more awesome and majestic than his grandfather had described. He reveled in the moment, again giving thanks to God for this experience. He raised his head to the sky and took a deep breath of sea air, allowing the wind full on his face.

"Thank you," he whispered. "Thank you."

He looked back to the sea, the fog rapidly dissipating like a curtain, revealing his grand prize. To his left, along the shoreline, at the base of a thick forest of trees, Uriah thought he could see the outline of a structure. Although he could not determine precisely what it was, he knew in his heart it was not indigenous to these surroundings.

He raced up the hill to gain a better vantage point. From there Uriah knew instantly the structure he was seeing was undoubtedly manmade. Was this the place his grandfather had told him about? Was this the magical land where the thoughts of God were sold? He would find out soon enough.

His heart raced with both excitement and fear. The pain in his neck had disappeared and he hastily gathered his belongings. For a moment thoughts of the terrible legends and stories of evil in the town, by the sea, crept into his mind. But the soothing words of his grandfather overruled these thoughts assuaging any fears.

"Believe in his words," he told himself.

Uriah judged his distance from the ocean at a minimum of five miles and the rocky uneven terrain would be less than accommodating. He was now out of food and he had gone nearly twenty four hours without water. The hike would prove daunting, but inside him he felt a strange knowingness. A level of certainty he had not felt in a long time.

With a new excitement, energy and vigor, Uriah donned his backpack and headed downhill toward the sea. The fog both in his mind and on the valley floor below had now lifted completely. He began his descent.

He had managed to maintain an even pace, but the pain of hunger had slowed him a bit. Occasionally thoughts of bandits, and flesh eating gangs would find their way back into his mind. "What if," he began each terrifying thought? But quickly he would erase them, choosing instead to rely on the words of his grandfather, those stories of Utopia and thoughts of God. He silently prayed again that these stories were true.

It had taken Uriah more than two hours to descend the hill. At the bottom, the ground had leveled out into an army of swampy reeds, stretching high above his head. He had not seen the reeds from above, due to the angle of his view from the cliffs peak. Uriah could hear the sound of ocean birds and the faint repetition of the tides, but the reeds obscured his view of the sea and everything beyond. Uriah feared what might be lying in the grass and was unsure of what direction to take. He knew it would be easy for him to become lost in this forest of reeds and he didn't know how long or how wide it would spread.

"Follow your heart," echoed the voice of his grandfather.

Uriah took a step toward the forest of reeds and felt the ground give way a few inches. Beneath his foot he felt a small depression in the soil. It was a groove about the width of a spade head. He recognized it immediately as a trail. Perhaps, he thought, it would lead him to the sea, and he would find a town, "the" town on the other side.

The sunken path was narrow and overgrown; it appeared to have not been used for many years. He would have to feel the path more than seeing it. With each three to four steps Uriah took, he was forced to brush aside armfuls of swamp grass in order to clear a place to step. He continuously had to re-find the trail, again and again. His walk was tedious and energy-consuming; yet, within a short time, he had managed to delve deep into the swampy bog.

Uriah turned to look back and could no longer see the spot where he had entered. His view was now completely cut off from all distinguishing landmarks, and his heart began to sink. He realized it would be difficult, if not impossible, to find his way out even with the few hours of daylight remaining. And if he were to find his way back from where he came, what then? He would once again be at the mercy of the wild, without either food or water. It was the sea or bust, and there was no turning back.

Uriah continued on as another hour passed, his thirst now overwhelming. He felt frustrated with the painstaking task of clearing the reeds. The pain in his stomach had reached his head, and he grew dizzy. Exhausted and starving, he thought to lie down and succumb to the tall reeds, knowing full well if he did, he would not get up again. His grandfather's words echoed in his head. He had told Uriah, the place where the thoughts of God are sold is not easy to reach, but it would be well worth the journey.

He pressed on, a foot at a time, forcing himself to move forward. "Just ten more steps," he said aloud. He would repeat this process over and again, "One, two, three, four, f-" and then finally, a clearing outside the grass. Uriah emerged from the reeds as if he had been reborn. He found himself standing on a flat expanse of grass and sand. He was free of the reeds, before him lay the ocean, now clearly visible.

Suddenly, he could hear the sounds of the surf and the squawk of the seagulls overhead, sounds which were strangely inaudible only seconds earlier. He took a moment staring at a body of water, so large; he could scarcely believe what he was witnessing. It stretched as far as he could see in every direction.

Several hundred yards to his left, he again, spotted the manmade structure he had seen from the hill. Now on level ground, he could clearly see it was a sign, giant and wooden, waving gently in the ocean breeze. The angle from where he stood had prevented him from seeing what, if anything was written on it.

The trail, from which he emerged, continued along the shoreline, from the forest of reeds directly toward the sign. Beyond the sign, the trail widened. Uriah could see it stretched about two hundred feet, past the sign, and angled toward the ocean before disappearing again into a patch of trees.

"That road must lead to the town in Grandfather's stories," he whispered to himself. "I pray it does," he added with a lump in his throat. "No matter what happens," thought Uriah, "at least I have seen this beautiful ocean." Uriah felt another burst of energy, and his pace quickened, as he continued along the path toward the sign, unaware of what lay beyond.

☐■ FOUR ■☐

The sign along the trail measured about six feet high by ten feet wide. It was firmly secured by two large posts buried in to the ground. The sign was weathered, but sturdy. It was obvious to anyone, that whoever built it had intended for it to be there a very long time.

Uriah could see there was something written on the sign as he approached. In large white letters, someone had painted the words,

"Welcome to Hope!
Please leave your baggage here."
In smaller letters just below it read,
"Source products sold here."

Uriah looked down the road into the swath of trees, almost expecting to see the blood thirsty hordes of cannibals of which he had been warned. But there was nothing but the shaded gravel and dirt. He could see more of the road now. It took a bend about a hundred, or more, yards from the sign in the direction of the coast. This has to lead to the town, he reasoned. Uriah took a few steps but thought better of it. Heeding the message on the sign, he dropped his backpack with his bedroll on the side of the road, attempting to conceal it beneath a few stones.

"Not that kinda' baggage son!"

Uriah spun toward the voice, to his right, behind a patch of trees just beyond the sign, stood a large man with steely blue eyes. He held a wide smile on his broad, sun reddened face.

"Who are you?" asked Uriah, visibly frightened.

"I was jus' gonna' ask you the same thin'," smiled the large man.

"Wh-where did you c-come from?" asked Uriah trying to harness his fear. For an instant he thought of running back up the trail, into the tall weeds from where he had come, but realized in his present state that he wouldn't make it far.

"I asked you who you are." Uriah said, trying to sound more forceful this time.

"I saw ya'," said the man ignoring Uriah's panicked queries. "You must be the fella' what slept up on the bluff last night. I was out here with my trusty lant'rn doin' ma' rounds and thought I spotted a shadow up yonder." The man motioned to the top of the hill. He had a strange drawl to his speech. Uriah had never heard anyone speak like this before.

The man emerged from the trees toward him. He was large and intimidating, but a smile covered his entire face which seemed to calm Uriah.

"Folks call me Tru," the man said, extending a large beefy hand.

Uriah didn't answer right away. He was busy calculating a possible escape route in his head. After a few seconds the man pressed on.

"Thought ya' might be a bit parched," he said, handing Uriah a canteen of water.

Without hesitation, Uriah snatched the canteen from the man and guzzled ravenously. It was the purest tasting water he ever had, and he quickly emptied the contents in a matter of seconds.

"Sorry I drank it all," Uriah said panting, handing the canteen back to the man.

"It's alright, young fella.' Plenty more where that came from. So you gotta' name or do I just call ya' hilltop?" asked the man.

"My name is Uriah," he said as he cautiously took Tru's hand.

"We thought ya' might come this way."

"We?" said Uriah shakily.

Tru nodded and motioned down the road, "Yup, you'll meet 'em soon nuff."

"What is this place?"

"Well," said Tru as he leaned down grabbing the strap from Uriah's pack, "since I takes it you can read, you musta' figured by now you was in Hope."

"Hope?" asked Uriah.

"Yup," said Tru, as he slung the bag over his shoulder, eyeing the young man somewhat cautiously.

"Question is what brought you here? Sides those kickers a' course," motioning to Uriah's feet. "I guess the old man'll figure it out soon nuff."

Uriah seemed not to notice Tru's suspicion. He was staring down the trail toward the bend in the road.

"Hope," he repeated again, this time to himself.

"You look like ya' could use a bathin' for sure," smiled Tru. "I bet some grub might be fairly welcome as well. Am I right?"

Uriah did not answer; he continued to stare down the road with a dazed expression, until Tru snapped his fingers in front of his face. "Ya' with me son?"

"Sorry," said Uriah coming to. "It's just that I believe this is the town of my grandfather's stories." I have been searching for this place since I was forced to leave my home. I have walked for weeks from the town of Kwo."

"That so? Never heard of it, but I'm sure it's ain't a nice place," chuckled Tru. "What say you tell us about it when once you get yerself cleaned and fed. Hopes' just a hop, skip and a step 'round that there bend. I know the old man'll wanna' see ya' soon fer sure."

Tru started walking, and Uriah followed a few steps behind.

"What about my baggage?" asked Uriah. "Shouldn't you leave my pack?"

Tru let out a hearty laugh, causing Uriah to flush with embarrassment.

"What's so funny?"

"I told ya' son, it ain't that kinda baggage. It means this kinda baggage up here," said Tru, pointing to his head.

"That kinda baggage ain't welcome." Tru continued walking again, his laughter echoed among the trees above them.

Uriah wasn't sure what "up here" meant. He thought his new friend might be having some fun with him, but he was too tired and too hungry to care much. He followed behind, walking toward a place called Hope.

□■ FIVE ■□

The two men turned at the bend in the road. It was another fifty yards before they walked out from the patch of forest into a clearing, at the end of the trail. Before them stood the town of Hope. It was nestled snugly between the trees and the ocean. To Uriah it was the most beautiful place his eyes had seen, and he could not imagine that a more perfect marriage between land and sea existed elsewhere in the world. In the background was the steep rocky cliff from which Uriah had descended. Directly in front of the cliffs lay an open expanse of grass. The grass was a dark, rich green color—a color Uriah had never before seen. In the middle of the field stood two small deer, their heads down, nibbling at the grass beneath them. Both deer paused a moment and looked up at Uriah, then immediately returned to their grazing. Tru saw Uriah's attention was fixated on the two fawns.

"They're safe here," said Tru. "They know there's healthy food for 'em and they won't be harmed. That's how we likes it, and as you can see, so do they. Yup," continued Tru, "we got rabbits, dogs, cows, goats and piggies, near a full zoo. We love the animals here and they like bein' here. They ain't mistreated."

Hope was in stark contrast to Kwo. There were no stone walls or barbed wire barricades. There were no guard towers overlooking the city. Instead of dilapidated buildings, there were beautiful two-story

29

solid structures and not a single one appeared to be in disrepair. There were no signs of neglect of any kind, and the streets and lawns were clean and neatly manicured. It was obvious to Uriah that each home had been treated with love and care. Fully blossomed flowers lined the stone walkways leading to each door. Uriah never knew a home could look so warm, and inviting.

The sidewalks were filled with people; each with a brightness and energy about them. They seemed free to roam where they pleased and smiled broadly to one another as they passed. Each held a sincere look of affection and kindness on their faces. These were not the flesh-eating beasts the Company had told the people about.

There were no visible signs of hunger. Each person looked filled with a contentment and peace foreign to Uriah. There were no starving souls asking for food, or money, or any visible signs of crime and poverty, as were so common on the streets of Kwo. It was a world Uriah had only dreamed of. He looked around with his mouth agape in awe and wonderment, and Tru smiled.

In the center of town stood a park. A small group of men and women stood inside an ornately decorated gazebo and began to sing. The sound too was like nothing Uriah had heard before.

"What is that?" he asked.

"They're singin' son. Ain't you never heard singin' 'fore? Oh, course not," said Tru, sheepishly.

Uriah thought a moment. It had been many years since he heard a melody of any kind.

Once Akuna had whispered a soft melody to him when they were just children, but singing had been outlawed long ago in his town. She had been reprimanded harshly for this act, and as a result, Akuna nor anyone else Uriah knew, was able to sing again.

"Here we go," said Tru excitedly. "This here's where yu'll stay."

Tru led Uriah to a beautiful pitched roof structure. It was white with blue trim and a red brick chimney ran along the side. Robust ivy vines, about two feet high, hugged the exterior of the front of the home. Uriah noticed many of the homes were painted in brightly colored pastels and each displayed the individual owner's personal expression through various decorations.

Off one end of Tru's porch was a magnificent view of the ocean. Water vessels of all kinds and sizes filled the harbor docks. The inside of the home was beautifully decorated with a variety of sculptures and paintings adorning each room and wall. Most were of landscapes and nature and each had a glow of warmth and serenity about them. In the back room was a plush bed with clean linen, and Uriah nearly wept at the thought of not having to sleep on the cold hard ground. He slowly scanned the room in wonder.

"Little hobby a' mine," said Tru, motioning to the paintings on the wall.

"They are very nice," said Uriah. "Are they worth much?" He was immediately embarrassed he had asked.

"They are ta' me," laughed Tru.

Uriah knew little of art. He was more touched by the creative expression of the man and his willingness to display such a personal side of himself. He knew in that moment he liked Tru very much.

"Bath's in the next room, help yerself," offered Tru, tossing Uriah a towel.

Uriah scrubbed away weeks of outdoor living from his body, languishing in the crystal-clear life-restoring water. He could grow used to bathing in a place which provided running water, he told himself.

Tru had also given Uriah a fresh set of his son's old clothes to wear.

"Can't promise you'll win any fashion shows with these here. Course, once ya' get some meat on yer bones, you'll grow inta' 'em just fine I suppose."

Uriah emerged from the washroom and could immediately smell the sweet summer fruit, browned potatoes, warm bread, a medley of jams, and just-squeezed juices, emanating from the kitchen. Tru was whistling a catchy melody while he prepared the food. He was smiling as usual, a blue cloth apron hung from his thick neck.

"Looks good on ya', near fits ya' too." Tru smiled proudly. "Sit and eat," he said, motioning to the chair and setting down a plate for Uriah. He guzzled down a glass full of the juice without hesitating. Tru had barely poured him a second glass when Uriah drank this glass as voraciously as the first. "You'll love my vittles; 'nother hobby a' mine. Yup, I loves to cook." Uriah seemed to pay no attention to Tru. He had already taken in his first full mouthful of food, eating as if a man possessed. Uriah then gobbled down nearly three helpings in large heaps, while Tru did most of the talking for the rest of the meal

"Yup, you'll fill out them duds out right fast," laughed Tru, watching Uriah scoop another fork load of food.

Uriah gulped down his food, barely pausing to chew. When he had finished, he sat back in his chair rubbing his belly and complained of a stomach ache.

"No surprise there," said Tru shaking his head. "I told ya' to slow down, but I suspect ya' couldn't hear me over the scrapin' of yer fork."

The pain in his stomach was secondary to the remorse he felt over his rush to gorge. He had failed to give thanks before his meal. It was an act denied him in his town, and he cherished the opportunity when he had the most meager of portions in the wild. He had already taken for granted the kindness and benevolence bestowed upon him, by a total stranger, and he vowed he would not let that happen again.

Tru looked over at Uriah and reasoned that a good night's rest was in order before meeting the old man. "Breakfast'll be on the table when you rise, son," he assured Uriah. "I suggest ya' take 'er down a notch or two when ya' grub again, if ya' can eat a' tall," he said giving Uriah a friendly wink.

Uriah nodded sheepishly and started for his room. He turned to Tru, his hand still rubbing his sore belly, "Will your son be coming back tonight?"

Tru looked at Uriah, his smile diminished slightly. "I keep prayin' son, I surely do."

He wanted to ask more about his son, but Tru told him again to get some sleep and Uriah was too tired to object.

That night Uriah slept as deep and sound as any person in history.

□■ SIX ■□

Uriah awoke to the sound of whistling. He emerged from the bedroom again to the smell of fresh fruit and warming dough in the kitchen. The aroma caused his stomach to sing like a pack of hungry hyenas. The dull pain of gorging from the night before had been replaced with a stabbing emptiness.

"Mornin'" smiled Tru cheerfully. "I reckon' you coulda' slept through a parade if one marched across yer pillow. Sorry if I was makin' nuff noise to wake the dead."

Uriah rubbed the sleep from his eyes. "What time is it?"

"Half noon nearly, I suspect, we don't much keep ta' time here. Hurry up and eat slow," chuckled Tru. "We'll head on over to the old man's, once you got some more fuel in ya'."

Uriah ate heartily again. He was careful to chew each spoonful, but more importantly he paused to give thanks and gratitude for his bounty. The last eighteen hours he had much to be grateful for, and he would not forget to acknowledge the source of his abundance this time.

Tru smiled warmly as Uriah bowed his head and he, too, followed suit.

After breakfast, the two men walked a short distance and arrived at the home of the old man. It was similar to the others, a two-story modest A-frame style home, overlooking the harbor. Inside, the furniture was all neatly arranged. More works of self-expressive art, adorned the walls and shelves of the home. Illuminating sunlight beamed in through every window in the home. The feel inside, to Uriah, was warm and inviting. Just as he had in Tru's home, he felt instantly welcome.

From a room near the back of the house emerged a man. Given how Tru referred to him, Uriah had expected him to be old and feeble with an arched back, leaning on a cane perhaps. Although Uriah guessed the man was nearly seventy, he was spry and energetic. A large, beaming smile covered his face, and his large green eyes sparkled with radiance.

"Welcome to Hope," said the man. "In spite of what Mister Tru here may have told you, my name is Percy, not Old Man." He took Uriah's hand in his. "You must be young Uriah from the mountaintop." Percy's voice was soft and steady and Uriah felt immediately at ease.

"Yes sir, I am," he said, as he looked at Tru, wondering what he may have told Percy while he slept.

"Percy if you will. Everyone here calls me Percy. Everyone here except this one," he said, waving his thumb in Tru's direction.

"You have a beautiful home, Percy."

"Thank you. I built it myself. In fact we all build our own homes here. With a little help of course," he said, throwing a smile at Tru.

The three men sat down in the living room making idle talk. Once comfortable, Uriah began to explain to the two men how he had been banished, from his town of Kwo, and forced to leave by the Company. He told how he had wandered through the wilderness in search of a place he wasn't certain existed. He spoke of the towns he had passed through, and how he was unwelcome in these places. The two men seemed particularly interested in these places. He also told of how Tru had found him.

He spoke of his grandfather's stories of this place, a magical town, not filled with the same pain and sorrow of his home. He talked of Akuna, and how he had been forced to leave her behind, and that one day he hoped to return for her.

"Tell me about this Company?" asked Percy.

Uriah told them everything he knew. The Company controlled all thoughts the people were allowed to think. They ruled the town of Kwo and others like it, with total dominance. He mentioned how the rulers forced the people to buy thoughts only from them. People were enslaved, living lives of ignorance, all languished in poverty and despair, due to the thoughts they were forced to think. Disempowering thoughts of ugliness, anger, and hatred were a few of the products that each citizen was required to own by law. No one was allowed to own any thoughts that the Company did not approve, and only those negative thoughts which caused adverse or chaotic behavior, were allowed. Failure to adhere to these laws would meet with swift and cruel punishment. Banishment from the safety of the city was Uriah's punishment.

He described how he had been turned out from his home for refusing to accept the thoughts of the Company. His grandfather said that he was someone who raised questions that those in power did not wish to answer. Uriah had always exhibited a resistance to purchasing the thoughts of the Company, and as he grew older, his resistance grew. Uriah struggled to adapt the hatred, greed, and jealousy, required by the Company—in his heart, he always believed there was something else.

He spoke of how he had been warned by the Company's leaders to buy thoughts only from them, how he must consume only what they provided. Still, Uriah continued his acts of free will and searched his conscience for the thoughts of God. His grandfather had pleaded with the authorities to not arrest Uriah, telling them that he was only a boy and that he was merely exhibiting the foolishness of youth. But, he could not conform, and rather than arrest him, he was banished to the outland. He said there were others like him, many were either imprisoned or put to death.

"They took everything from me...except this," he said, presenting his journal from his pocket. "I began keeping it a few years ago. It is filled with the thoughts I wish to think and act upon, that were forbidden me, in Kwo. My dreams and goals, my wish to express love. I was forced to keep it hidden from the Company, or it would be burned, and I would be arrested immediately." Uriah did not feel compelled to share the details of his journal nor did the men ask. His latest entry, a desire to marry Akuna, was for his eyes only.

"Did this Company ever speak of Hope?" asked Percy.

Uriah nodded. "They said this was a place of evil and death. They said all who came here never returned."

"But you didn't believe them?" asked Percy.

"Something inside me told me you must be here," said Uriah, pointing to his heart. "That my grandfather's stories were true! It's almost as if," he hesitated, "as if I have been summoned to this place."

Percy sat back and shot a quick glance toward Tru. The two men smiled at one another and then turned their attention back to Uriah.

"Had my grandfather not told me of this place, I would have wandered aimlessly until I was consumed by hungry animals or worse."

Uriah paused a moment. He had always been told the lands outside of Kwo were fraught with danger, and yet he experienced none during his journey to this place. Like most people, he simply accepted the legends of evil, handed down by his grandfather, and the authorities of the Company. He suspected his grandfather, too, had simply accepted the stories he was told. This was how it was with all people in Kwo, each programmed to believe in only the worst rumors without question, regardless of merit or references.

Uriah wondered why it was easy for people to believe in only the negative. And inside, he now questioned whether the things he was told about the wilds were true, or yet another propaganda campaign, lobbied by the Company. He would revisit this theory later, he reasoned.

"My grandfather told me to follow the brightest star towards the sea," he continued. "Yesterday morning, that is when I saw your sign from the mountaintop. That is when I met Tru." Uriah fell silent for a moment, he had not realized his fists had been clenched the entire time he spoke, and he now relaxed them. "I believe I would not have lasted another day, for certain, had I not found your town."

"Did your grandfather tell you anything else?"

"Only that this was a place where joy and freedom to be who you wish to be was possible." Uriah looked to both men. They gave no expression from which he could get a read.

After a few seconds, Uriah could take the silence no longer and finally asked, "Was my grandfather right?"

"Yes," answered Percy without hesitation. Tru looked at Percy and smiled.

"I know we are asking many questions, but it is important for us to determine how you came to be here, Uriah," said Percy, leaning in. "What you call the Company has been known to send spies to Hope. Their goal, as you may know, is for everyone to consume only what they offer. They would like nothing more than to infect our town and make it their own."

Uriah sat up in his chair. He was about to object to the perceived accusation he might be guilty of espionage, when Percy put his hand up to calm him.

"Relax son, we know you are not a spy, Uriah. There is truth in your words and a belief in your heart. We can see that very clearly. You have the energy of love, and it is sincere."

Tru nodded in agreement. "Heck, I nearly knowed it the second I layed eyes on ya.'"

"Now, did your grandfather tell you how this Company came to be?" Percy asked.

Uriah shook his head. "No, he said the Company was already in power when he was a boy and that his grandfather had told him of this place. He felt it has been here for a long time. I think," he said searching, "the stories of this place must have been handed down over many generations. My grandfather often wondered how we have gotten so far from God, but he knew it didn't happen overnight."

"That is true," smiled Percy. "Hope has been here a very long time, since the beginning. In fact it has been here even longer than the Company. Most are unaware of this."

Percy leaned back in his chair. He took a pipe from his pocket and packed it full. He lit the pipe and the aroma of sweet smelling tobacco filled the room. Tru opened the window allowing the smoke to escape and immediately Uriah could hear children playing just outside.

Percy blew out a large puff of smoke. "Do you hear that?" he asked rhetorically.

Uriah nodded.

"Those children you hear are the reason this town was created. With imagination and inspiration, they can be all that they wish to be." Percy leaned forward looking directly into Uriah's eyes, "They are not subject to the rules and limitations of any tyrannical company. They are our greatest hope for true change."

Uriah stood and went to the window to see the children playing. He could see there was much sharing and cooperation involved; there was laughter, truth, and innocence in their actions.

Uriah did not know the game the children played; in Kwo, the Company had forbid any form of sharing or joyful togetherness, games of any kind were forbidden. The laughter outside made Uriah long for Akuna and a life he knew that was possible.

"Why did I have to feel different than everyone else Kwo?" asked Uriah, never taking his eyes off the children. "I have always felt as if there is more. No one was happy in Kwo, but it was all I knew. If I had just stayed in Kwo and bought the ideas like everyone else, at least I would still be near to Akuna."

"Then what?"" asked Percy. "You would be with a woman, but unable to express your love to her. Here in Hope you are able to purchase all the love, imagination, and care you can afford and express it freely. Here you may buy all that serves you, young Uriah."

Uriah wished to know why people were not free to buy from who they chose. He wanted to know why the Company had so much power and influence.

Percy leaned back in his chair and inhaled deeply from his pipe. "I would like you to get comfortable, Uriah, for I have a story to tell you. One I think you might find very interesting."

Then Percy blew out a ring of smoke and began to speak.

□■ SEVEN ■□

"Do you know where your thoughts come from, Uriah?" began Percy.

Uriah nodded. "Thoughts are a product of the Company."

The old man smiled and shook his head slightly. "For millennia, man did not know where his thoughts originated. They were believed to be merely invisible threads of energy, which we pulled into our minds. These energy threads determine our feelings and behaviors and essentially how we act and how we live. They are the genesis of what we become in life. We pull these unseen threads into the world of the seen. Everything you see in your world is a result of your thoughts, the thoughts of God or the thoughts of the Company. Your every thought Uriah, affects the world." Percy pointed toward the open window, "And the thoughts of those children and others like them are creating a world of the future."

"So where do our thoughts come from?"

"We have come to learn that thoughts are sold to us by God," answered Percy.

Uriah gave no reaction.

"God created a company in which to dispense these thoughts," continued Percy. "He named His company

45

the Source. It was the Source of all creation, especially our thoughts."

"You felt called here cause ya' must realize the power of these here thoughts a' God," said Tru. "Ya' knew there was more than what the Company in yer town offered. These here thoughts is what compelled you to come here ta' us."

"Many, many years ago," continued Percy, "God saw that man had become a species of consumers. We consumed anything and everything possible, goods, products, services, information, and nearly all the world's irreplaceable natural resources. Mankind was a beast of consumption, crawling over one another to buy all things. We were like ants in a puddle of sweet juice. The one thing we have always had in abundance was our thoughts, those flashes of brilliance which travel through our cerebral cortex like an intergalactic meteor shower. We consume not only from the seen, but the unseen as well, those things which are truly limitless in scope and scale. Some believe individuals purchase some sixty thousand thoughts per day, per person! From the beginning, God has sold mankind his thoughts, only man didn't know where these thoughts came from. God sold thoughts, ideas, inspiration, and all the things that enrich our lives and serve us. The inspiration to sculpt, to paint, to dance, to bring joy and passion to others, to learn or to explore, to give, to love, to show compassion, they are all offerings of the Source. The Source sells all those products which benefit mankind, from childhood dreams of space travel to the creation of all love and beauty and beyond."

Percy glanced out the window and smiled at the laughter of the children outside. "The Source sells us our purpose in life and also the talents and abilities, in which to fulfill that purpose. To man, earth was a canvas and his thoughts the brush. A brush he could use to design whatever life he chose, if only were to purchase his thoughts from the Source." Percy paused and smiled at Uriah, "And pay the required fee of course."

"Fee, what fee does God require?" asked Uriah, puzzled.

"He simply requires a payment of faith, thanks, and action. It is a small payment to accept our dreams. And with this payment, we receive accomplishment in the seemingly impossible. Whatever we choose to have in life can be ours, if it be for the betterment of all. We must simply pay the asking price."

"Why doesn't God just give us what we want?" Uriah became instantly embarrassed by his question, but Percy showed no hint of contempt on his face.

"Happiness and fulfillment in this life is never free, Uriah. All things of value must be paid for in full. Besides, God knows we are capable of accomplishing all He offers us. Otherwise, He never would have asked us to buy in the first place. But it is up to us to take the action."

"Why did ya' choose to bow yer head 'fore breakfast?" asked Tru. "Ya' can't tell me you was taking a nap. No sir, you was giving thanks fer yer

47

meal and that there gratitude only increases more a' the same."

Uriah looked at Tru and nodded an unspoken understanding and then continued asking more about the thoughts of God.

"But how does God sell us these thoughts?"

"His methods vary greatly, the same as your Company in Kwo."

"Only different products for sure," said Tru.

"Just as there is no limit to His offerings, there is no limit to the ways in which He sells," said Percy, continuing. "He approaches us through personal philosophies, through book passages, words and phrases, people we encounter, animals, nature; sometimes a whisper in the ear, the list goes on. Sometimes through our journal writing," he said motioning to Uriah's journal. "Any celestial tap on the shoulder inspiring us to a higher calling or keener sense of awareness can and is used by the Source."

"Any nudge from above is right," chimed Tru. "*God winks* is what I calls 'em. Heck, I suspect he even goes door-to-door a' times." Tru alone chuckled at this.

"I am certain from what you have told me, you yourself have been approached by God, young Uriah," smiled Percy, "and have already purchased a few of His ideas."

A puzzled look formed across Uriah's face. "If you hadn't I do not believe you would be here with us now, said Percy."

"I do not remember…" began Uriah, when Percy cut him off.

"Your grandfather perhaps? God has no boundaries in His approach to sell His ideas. I believe your grandfather's stories were a vessel for His products."

"And you the one which bought 'em," said Tru. "Is why yer here now for sure."

"So many thoughts are being sold to us," said Uriah shaking his head. "How do we know what to do when they come so fast?"

"It wasn't always like this," said Percy. "God also sold us on the notion of slowing down our minds. He sold us things like prayer and meditation. Practices like these make room for a place of peace within our minds so we can create happiness in our lives. All you have to do is quiet your mind, ask God what's for sale today, and then listen for the answer. But humans wanted more of everything and faster."

Percy took his pipe, emptied the charred contents into a can by his side, and placed it on the table beside him. "People got so used to buying thoughts from the Company, they weren't aware they were even buying them at all. Thoughts flew in so fast they just kind of came to folks and they took them in and made them their own."

Uriah sat back in his chair. He understood the concept of buying ideas from God. It was after all what the Company in Kwo was all about preventing. Only ideas, notions and products from the Company were permitted and thoughts not from the Company were forbidden. Those thoughts which were not of jealousy, greed, envy, hate, or the like, were disallowed inside the town limits.

After a moment, Uriah asked the question his grandfather had wondered for as long as he could remember.

"How then did people get so far from the thoughts of God?"

Percy shrugged, "Maybe we got lazy," he said flatly.

"For starters," quipped Tru. "Besides, God doesn't force folks to purchase His goods, that ain't how He operates."

"I guess trusting God's goods, thanking Him and taking action on His offers was too much to ask from man. Growth and enlightenment were available to all. Human potential and lives of enrichment were there for the taking. Peace in the world was possible. Each individual was the master of his or her destiny and then..." Percy paused. He looked down at the floor and the creases in his brow became deep and furrowed. "I guess we just started taking God for granted and expected His products for free. Maybe we felt the price He was asking was too steep."

Uriah's gaze also fell to the floor, matching Percy's.

"Which is why none seemed to take notice a' the danger which lie ahead," added Tru. "It crept in quiet-like, stealthily and indiscriminate. Heck, I suspect most folks never see'd it comin'."

"What danger?" Uriah asked.

"A danger you are very familiar with," said Percy. "That's when the Company, like the one you have in Kwo, showed up. You see, Uriah, it was then when man met God's competition."

EIGHT

"Originally he worked for the Source," Percy began.

"God didn't work alone, as some might suspect. He had a staff and, as I told you, His methods were limitless. That's where this worker of His comes in, an employee of the Source. He was good too, one of God's best salesmen in fact. He was the muse, the catalyst of ideas, the provider of dreams and the seller of the tools in the attainment of all mans' goals. He worked in the new product line for the Source as well, a real genius at developing new empowering thoughts for man. He would create new ideas to sell to man and God would give His stamp of approval, as it were. If it was of a benefit to the individual and for the good of humanity, it went out on the market. He was never turned down either. That is until…" Percy hesitated a moment. He looked up at the ceiling, as if searching for the words, "Well let's just say this super salesman got a bit ambitious."

Outside the children let out a loud burst of laughter. Tru got up and headed toward the window. Uriah expected him to close it, but instead, he flung the shutters open wider and pulled the drapes apart as far as they would extend.

"It's like music to tha' ears," said Tru smiling. "He was right," thought Uriah. Their laughter *was* music to his ears and gave him joy in his heart. He was glad Tru had not closed the window.

Once Tru was seated, Percy began again.

"One day, this fella', this salesman for the Source, brought a new product to God. A product he called doubt. See I guess this salesman was never entirely sold on the idea that we carbon-based life forms with pedestrian minds and clunky bodies should have anything God was willing to sell us. 'If it was going to be this way,' reasoned the salesman, 'then why not open up an entire new product line?' There was so much more he could offer to the people. Humans were fertile soil, an untapped market, after all, and this new product practically sold itself. They would surely buy all products the Source offered. And this doubt thing would be a big seller. But God refused. He didn't care much for doubt. He wanted only self-empowering life-enriching ideas sold to man."

"If only they pay the asking price," Uriah added. He quickly leaned back, embarrassed that he had presumed to understand.

"It's fine," said Percy smiling at him. "And you are absolutely correct!"

"You're free to express yerself here," Tru assured him. "Es' what we're all about."

"You see, God sold to humans only those mentally or spiritually empowering beliefs, and doubt didn't qualify."

"And that didn't sit well with this salesman," added Uriah, with a sudden sureness.

"Correct again!" beamed Percy.

"Looks like someone jus' bought themselves a heap a' confidence," said Tru laughing.

"This salesman was an ambitious soul," Percy continued ignoring Tru. "He wanted expansion at all costs. And when God said no to this doubt product, he immediately quit the Source. He quit, taking several top level executives with him and started his own company. He would start his own product line, one that in time would outsell even the Source."

"That's the Company, this fellers' comp'ny what runs things in yer town a' Kwo," added Tru.

"He named this company EGO. It stood for Edging God Out."

"It's what ya' call an acronym," boasted Tru.

"And that's been precisely the goal of this company since the beginning, edging God out. It's been pretty darn successful too." Percy gave Uriah a crooked sympathetic smile," Of course I don't have to tell you."

Uriah had never heard it explained quite like this before. Whatever theories he had heard had happened long ago, stories that began long before he was born, long before in fact his grandfather was born, and these versions had all been watered down through the passage of time.

"How has this Company been able to successfully sell these ideas for so many years?"

"They have a hotshot sales team. Some are spirits, of sorts..." Tru went silent and looked to Percy to finish his thought and said finally, "Course they got humans workin' for 'em too, loads of 'em."

"In fact for many centuries now," continued Percy, "mankind has been the Company's best sales team. They have continued to share the products of EGO with one another."

"Sorta' word a' mouth advertising," if you will," added Tru. "Sellin' each other fear, doubt, anger, all those lovely things," Tru said sarcastically.

"But, then there are those who have continued to rebel against the products of EGO, men like you," added Percy.

"Thank Him for that," added Tru, pointing his finger upward.

The laughter outside had grown faint. Uriah could still hear the children playing, but it seemed they had taken their game elsewhere. He was honored that Percy and Tru had trusted him enough to share this history with him. They had given validation to many things he had felt over the years, but could not explain. He had always sensed that his life, and the lives of those he knew, was marching on woefully unfulfilled. Knowing the Company and purchasing only the thoughts and ideas offered by the Company had always somehow felt wrong and incomplete, even when he was forced to buy all the thoughts that the Company was selling. He was anxious to learn all he could, about where he had come from, and particularly more of what the Source had to offer. Soon thoughts of rescuing Akuna began to dance through his mind, and his questions took on an enthusiastic sense of urgency.

"Was there a price charged to man?" he asked.

"That was the greatest hook of all," answered Percy. "EGO claimed to charge absolutely nothing for their products." Percy made a circle with his thumb and forefinger to emphasize his point. "EGO claimed to give out their products free to man, sort of a trial offer, so to speak."

"But there was a price, wasn't there?" Uriah asked rhetorically.

"Yes," Percy answered. "There was in fact a heavy price for buying from EGO. Although people thought the products from EGO were free, they ended up paying a heavy price much later in life. The price they paid was lives filled with regret, unfulfilled dreams, unaccomplished goals and unquenched passions. Their God-gifted talents and purposes withered from atrophy on the vine of life. It was like a malevolent line of credit man never knew existed. At the end of each life, payment became due. And for most, it was too late."

"And believe you me," quipped Tru, "at the end of each life, EGO always comes a collectin'."

"Is that how they have gotten so powerful?" asked Uriah.

"That is one reason," answered Percy. "But there were other factors in play. EGO became powerful right from the beginning because they were never idle. They worked non stop creating so-called new and improved thoughts and ideas. What their product line lacked in quality, they made up for in salesmanship. They introduced their product in a casual, easy manner. They sold so subtlety, as Tru mentioned, most people were unaware they were being sold. They would sell man those thoughts and ideas that he didn't know he didn't need."

"Thoughts such as doubt," added Tru.

"I know this well," Uriah said. "All citizens of Kwo are required to own their share of doubt."

"It's no wonder," said Percy. "Doubt, their initial product was a popular and highly addictive substance. Once it was on the market, folks bought it in bulk."

"How did they sell it?" Uriah asked.

"Good question. Today it's sold as thoughts similar to the methods God uses to sell us His ideas. EGO basically copied His formula. They would follow up behind God with a tempting counter offer to the Source. All thoughts and ideas offered by God are of great value. If they weren't, EGO would not care to sell you thoughts to prevent their fulfillment. When the Source sold an idea to man, EGO instantly pitched doubt. Suddenly man began to have thoughts such as, 'I can't,' or 'It will never work,' or 'It's impossible,' and so on, until it began to consume his mind. These were thoughts man had never had before, but they soon became ubiquitous in his thinking."

Percy sat back and took a deep relaxing sigh, "There was a time when man used to buy those thoughts which made him happy and fulfilled…and now," he said shaking his head, "now he buys all the thoughts which leave him empty and saddened."

"Why did man keep buying?"

"As I said, doubt was addictive and very powerful. EGO sold it under the guise as an insurance policy of sorts, a protection against failure, if you will. If you doubt you can accomplish a task, you can easily talk yourself out of even attempting said task. Soon people everywhere were saying, 'I'm glad I didn't try that.'"

"Doubt," continued Percy, "didn't keep people from failing, it kept them from ever trying. And the more altruistic the endeavor, the more vigorous EGO pitched this product of doubt."

"Doubt kept folks from getting' clear on what they wanted," Tru added. "And those executives over at EGO loves confusion. Heck, chaos is them fellers' pillow."

Uriah knew doubt well. Although any expression of love had been outlawed in Kwo, doubt was the main reason he continually found himself unable to lean in for that first kiss with Akuna, that and his fear of expressing love in Kwo. It had kept him from asking her to dance or to take a walk under the stars. Since he had known her, it had kept him from telling her what he truly felt for her.

Doubt had kept him from singing, what he felt in his heart, and from writing what was in his soul for many years. Buying the doubt day-after-day and year-after-year was why all the townspeople in Kwo lived in misery. Percy was right, doubt didn't prevent people from failing; it kept them from ever trying. By purchasing enough doubt, they believed it would keep them safe and comfortable. They found themselves disregarding the life that could be, in return, for the unhappy familiarity of what was. And after years of buying from the Company, the people had unwittingly forfeited their right to choose. They were forced to buy only what the Company would sell. In Kwo and as in many towns it was difficult to know how many songs went unsung. It was equally difficult to know how many books went unwritten, how many paintings went unpainted, how many businesses failed to start, how many soufflés went unbaked, and how many romances failed to blossom…because of doubt. It was just as the Company of EGO wanted.

"EGO had many varieties of doubt as well," Percy began again. "Self doubt, doubt in others' abilities, doubt in God's good graces, doubt in God's products and their existence. Even doubt in the existence of God himself. After buying doubt, it was a short jump to inadequacy."

"Sort of an addendum to doubt," said Tru.

"That's right. Inadequacy had man believing he wasn't good enough, even if he did try. It went hand-in-hand with doubt and crippled many lives."

Uriah shook his head knowingly. Although he wasn't always familiar with all the titles of the Company's products, he certainly understood their uses. He had seen the looks of many of his friends and neighbors. They were looks of despair and uncertainty. He could almost feel their inadequacy as he passed them on the street as he was sure they could feel his.

Percy explained to Uriah that doubt and inadequacy were only the beginning. EGO had created many products to sell to people. The products were designed to trip up mankind at every turn. And these products flew off the shelves, almost as fast, as EGO could manufacture them.

□■ NINE ■□

"It wasn't always about the products themselves," Percy said. "Oh sure, they were damaging for certain, but it was what these things led to. That was the real blow to mankind." Percy leaned back in his chair and again, looked up, as if searching for answers. "You know, I often wonder if even EGO knew how successful they would become and how much damage they could do to the Source."

Percy shook his head as if to clear this thought. "Anyway," he continued, "EGO sold a whole line of products. Once doubt and inadequacy were in place, it was an easy sell. Lower the esteem of humanity and you can pretty much sell them anything that they think might make them feel better in the moment, or at least keep them from more pain."

"That were a big hook fer sure," said Tru. "EGO told folks they could avoid pain by buyin' doubt. Course they didn't tell them they wasn't gonna' be livin' nor growin' anymore neither."

A light breeze blew in through the open window. Tru got up, this time to close it shut. The children had since taken their game out of sound and sight, spreading their laughter elsewhere, Uriah supposed. Before shutting the window, Uriah noticed how Tru lifted his face to the sun above and closed his eyes. He was silent for a moment, and Uriah could see Tru was giving thanks to God for the warmth and nurturing that the sun was providing.

"Pride," continued Percy, snapping Uriah back to the room, "was one such item. Pride with a side order of arrogance was a product designed to deny the positive impact of the Source. Pride told man he was the true origin of all his creative genius and accomplishments. Pride blinded man to the greatness of God. Who needed to pay God His due when pride and arrogance gave man all the credit? EGO sold man pride which told him to place himself on a pedestal and then sold him the pedestal as well. By purchasing enough pride, man no longer needed God, for he now believed he was the Source of all things. Pride soon toppled men from heads of households to heads of state without discrimination or preference."

"Ever hear of a fella' by the name a' George Custer?" Tru asked.

Uriah shook his head. Reading and the studying of history had been a few of the many things that were forbidden in Kwo.

"You can read of 'em, if ya' like." Tru walked over to the bookshelf, grabbed a book and handed it to Uriah. "He was an American Indian fighter a long ways back," he continued, settling back into his chair. "Got famous most for the way he died. Anyway it weren't Sioux arrows what kilt' him an' his men at a place called Little Big Horn. It were pride and arrogance. Ugly pride gets folks killed for sure. It don't always affect jus' one. You jus' read about it, you'll see."

It was knowledge Uriah hoped to gain. He could do that here in Hope. He would read about historical facts, great heroes, and exotic places around the world. He could also study music, geography, and art as well as any other subjects his heart desired.

He had a lifetime of learning and growing to make up for, but his mind and thoughts never drifted far from Akuna. He wished she were here with him now, but he knew he could not force her to leave Kwo. She had to want to leave. He knew she was a buyer of the products of EGO and was imprisoned in the fear and doubt she was forced to consume. With every item Percy described, Uriah could see Akuna's face. She, like so many others, were subjects to all the Company sold.

Percy emphasized how, over many generations, people had simply accepted the pattern of buying these thoughts. They accepted their fate as to what they were forced to consume and lived lives of utter desperation, void of creative expression, or fulfillment of any kind.

"The quality of a man's life is the sum total of the quality of his thoughts," said Percy. "EGO has always known this and has used it in an attempt to destroy and enslave mankind." Neither of the men found it necessary to again note how successful EGO had become in their efforts.

The three men continued to talk for more than an hour. Percy spoke more on the product line of EGO, Uriah recognizing them one-by-one, as he described the characteristics of each. He spoke of how EGO sold man judgment and how its power heightened in accordance with the level of ignorance of the user. The more uninformed the owner of judgment, the more effective it became. It allowed man to delve deeply into the lives of others; completely neglecting his own matters. Through judgment, he would become distracted from attending to his own concerns. It was an excellent item for separating and dividing man. Once judgment hit the market, it quickly became an unstoppable entity. Man used it to separate from one another in every way possible. Eye color, hair color, height, weight, education, mannerisms, personal habits—there was seemingly no end to the ways in which man could use his newly bought judgment. If it could be labeled, it would fall under the umbrella of judgment.

Tru, never at a loss to provide Uriah historical specifics, told him of the deadly effects of judgment. He told him how long ago, judgment, with the purchase of fear, had caused the death of many innocent women to be burned and hung for crimes of witchcraft.

"Got a book on it too, when yer ready," said Tru.

"I know this product well," Uriah said. "It is used a great deal against the many homeless in my town."

According to Percy, there seemed to be no end to the line of merchandise available at EGO. If God sold inspiration or intuition, EGO sold a product to counter act this. One which would distract man from all intentions, Source related. Ironically, EGO, like man, seemed limited only by imagination.

"These thoughts," said Percy, "these invisible frequencies resonate throughout the universe. These vibrations can cause either chaos or peace, depending on where they originate. This is true whether they buy from either the Source or the EGO."

"Why didn't people stop what was happening?" Uriah asked. "How did they let it get this far?"

"By the time they knew what was happenin,' it were too late," answered Tru. "Besides, they wasn't sure how to stop EGO by then anyways."

"These thoughts sold by EGO, as I said, were damaging alone to individuals, but the cumulative affect they had on the world's population was devastating."

Uriah nodded. He had absorbed much information, but was eager to learn all they were willing to tell him.

"Things began to slowly erode," said Percy. "By the time man realized what had happened, buying thoughts from EGO had become uncontrollable. It took less than a few generations before buying from EGO was not only accepted, but it became expected. EGO steadily took control of the people's thoughts. Over the years, the quality of life for many slowly dwindled. Once people finally did realize their lives had spun out of control, they began to blame all their problems on God. They were looking for a scapegoat."

"Why blame God?" Uriah asked puzzled "You said God only sold those thoughts which are good for us."

"Because God is the creator of thought," answered Percy. "Most people chose to blame God for the condition of their lives rather than take responsibility for buying from EGO."

"B'sides," added Tru, "they'd had to buy their responsibility from the Source and EGO weren't allowin' that ta' happen. What ya' might call a catch twenny two, so to speak."

"Man's been blaming God ever since," said Percy. "But things they were about to get worse, much worse."

□■ TEN ■□

Outside, the sun was slowly slipping beneath the horizon. The three men had spent nearly all the daylight hours talking.

The three decided to break for dinner. Tru prepared a meal of assorted vegetables for them all, incorporating a wide spectrum of colors from the vegetable family. There were the leafy greens of lettuce and kale, orange from carrots, yellow corn, and the purple of squash, red peppers, and whitened beets, in addition to a perfectly grilled slice of the local lake fish. Cubes of pineapple were served for a sweet treat and digestive aid.

The fruit and vegetables had a freshness Uriah had never before experienced. They did not have the synthetic flavor to which he had become accustomed to in Kwo. Percy told him there was a large garden in Hope, where all the fresh fruits and vegetables were organically grown. Each person attended to their own designated section of the garden. To Uriah, vegetables had never tasted so delicious.

"Where did you learn to prepare meals like this?" Uriah asked.

"Like I tole ya', is a hobby a' mine. Always had a love for fixin' food," answered Tru.

"Never was allowed to get around to it b'fore comin' here tho'. Here in Hope, I haves the freedom to express my love and talents for those things in my heart. Cooking and preparing meals from my heart was what I always enjoyed, jus' weren't always allowed to express my passion, if ya' knows what I mean. And I'm sure ya' do at that."

Uriah understood immediately what Tru meant. There were many things in Uriah's life which he was forbidden to express. His feelings for Akuna were the main things he was denied. As feelings of love and commitment were forbidden in Kwo, marriage and children were solely for the propagation of the species and nothing more. His writing stifled, as well. His grandfather taught him to read and write at a very young age. He studied in secret, late at night, and always carefully hid his letters away from the Company. His thoughts of learning were locked tight from the prying eyes of the community and the authorities.

The three men sat down to eat. Uriah looked around nervously before bowing his head. He then closed his eyes to offer thanks. Percy and Tru watched him closely and smiled, and then they too gave thanks for their bounty.

"I noticed that this mornin'," said Tru dishing out a plate to each of them. "Did your gran'pop teach ya' that?"

Uriah thought about it for a moment. He had shown gratitude for the precious gift of food, for as long as he could remember, and had forgotten where he had learned this behavior.

"I'm not sure," Uriah finally answered. "It's just something I have always felt in my heart to do, to show gratitude to my provider. I have hidden my thanks for many years and was never allowed to express it."

Percy smiled at Uriah. "As Tru mentioned, giving thanks for God's gifts only increases His grace. That is what those who buy from EGO have forgotten and it is why EGO could not enslave you. God and the products of the Source have never left you alone."

"I still don't understand," said Uriah. "Why do so many continue to buy the thoughts that do not serve them?"

"There are many reasons," answered Percy. "Each of us must decide for ourselves. Always remember this," he said leaning in to Uriah, "when God sells you the idea you are magnificent, who are you to believe you are not?"

The men spent the remainder of the meal laughing and talking of lighter subjects. Each shared stories of their favorite days. Percy, the day he found Hope; Tru, the birth of his son, and Uriah, the day he met Akuna. Percy mentioned the Source would provide many more favorite moments, as long as each was willing to pay the asking price.

"The future is as bright as our hearts can afford," said Percy, raising his cup and toasting the table.

After the meal, the three returned to the sitting area. Uriah expected Percy to tell him more of the EGO and the Source, but the feeling had grown light and festive. Uriah knew he had more to tell him and sensed the subject, too dark and heavy; after all they had already talked about. Tomorrow Percy and Tru would begin again, not wanting to give Uriah too much at once.

Before turning in, Percy showed Uriah the rest of his extensive library. The collection of books, numbered more than a thousand. The exact number Percy was not certain, as new books were frequently added. The library covered nearly every topic available, history, fiction, fantasy, romance, science fiction, biographies—anything which a young, eager mind wished to absorb.

"Books are our connection to the past," mused Percy. "This collection is more valuable than anything I own, with the exception of my mind of course. They teach us, entertain us, and through their words, God offers us the product of imagination. They can take us wherever we wish to go, if only we are buying. But not all knowledge of the Source can come from books."

"What do you mean?" asked Uriah.

"There are some things about the Source you must discover for yourself. Things we cannot teach you, something you must find in here," said Percy pointing to his chest. Percy's words caused Uriah to once again reach into his coat pocket and lightly thumbed the cover of his journal. He thought he knew what Percy meant.

The journal was worn and tearing at the seams. But it contained his most cherished thoughts, and those thoughts of Akuna, and of the life he knew in his heart that existed outside of Kwo. The journal had served as his lifeline to another world.

He looked over and eyed Percy's tomes, eager to gobble them up, but none would become as cherished as his own thoughts.

"Where did you get them all?" Uriah asked in amazement.

"I have collected most of them myself. Many have been given to me by the people here in Hope. It is an archive of education and imagination, and they remain here with me for safekeeping. All people here in Hope are welcome and encouraged to read as much as they like."

"Books are outlawed in Kwo," said Uriah. "You can be imprisoned for having one."

Percy nodded knowingly. "That is because the Source sells us ideas through books. EGO does not want the community to educate themselves nor begin to learn of thoughts offered by God. EGO wants everyone to believe they are insignificant. And as long as the people buy from them, they will continue to believe just that. That is why this collection of books is so valuable. These may be among the few that are left in the world."

Percy offered Uriah his choice of books. He chose an adventure story about a young man's journey spanning several continents in search of happiness and love. He would read these along with the book Tru had given him. There would be plenty of time for reading the books in Hope, and Uriah wanted to read them all.

"Excellent choice; just remember to read between the lines," joked Percy, handing Uriah the book.

Uriah wasn't sure what he meant, but was embarrassed to reveal this. He nodded and quickly shoved the book in his back pocket.

"Careful with that," said Tru behind him. "Them books is as valuable as air, in some cases."

It was getting late, and Uriah had grown tired. He thanked Tru for the meal and Percy for the books, assuring them he would read them right away.

"You can stay here tonight," offered Percy. "We'll finish our story tomorrow. For now you need your rest."

Before turning in for the night, Uriah gave thanks to God for that day's offerings. He was growing less fearful in his display of gratitude, with each instance. He felt the moments of hiding his thoughts and his feelings, from the Company, were over. In Hope, he was beginning to experience how he could easily purchase the thoughts of God and was more than willing to pay the price.

That night Uriah had a dream. He was back in Kwo with Akuna. He dreamed that he told her how he loved her and how he wanted to spend his life with her. He told her he wanted to have a family with her.

They would raise their children in a place called Hope. It was a village by the sea, where the people were free to buy imagination, inspiration, and faith. Their children could be whatever they wanted and would buy those thoughts, which would enrich them. They could learn together and find a new way to live—an empowering way—living by the grace of the products of the Source. They would be free to grow and accept all the thoughts and ideas that God offered. All that was required of her was to purchase a belief, in a better life outside of Kwo, from the Source, and her willingness to pay God His due. Before Akuna could answer, Uriah awoke from his dream.

□■ ELEVEN ■□

The three men had retaken the same seats from the day before. After another night of restful sleep, Uriah was beginning to get his legs under him. He was young and strong but his time in the wilderness, coupled with the continuous exposure to the elements, had taken its toll on him. The combination of healthy meals, restful sleep, and God-offered thoughts were proving to be a just remedy, and his eagerness to learn intensified as his body repaired.

"You mentioned yesterday that things had gotten worse," began Uriah, as the three men started to talk after their morning meal.

Percy chuckled at his enthusiasm and began to tell him the story. He reminded Uriah how the salesmen of EGO had followed closely behind the Source, in an attempt to sell man those thoughts, contrary to God's intentions. He told him how when the Source offered thoughts of peace, EGO followed closely behind, in an effort, to sell anger and disharmony. When God offered love, EGO countered with hate and indifference. When the Source offered the product of forgiveness, EGO used all its resources to sell the tempting product of revenge.

"As we said earlier, people found it easier to purchase the thoughts they believed would keep them safe and comfortable," said Percy. "Slowly and steadily, man stopped buying from the Source altogether. EGO began to control through laws, rules and regulations. The use of words such as love and compassion were forbidden as you know. They took control of the world economy and eventually the military. From there it was a slippery slope to total control of the thoughts of the people. The goal of EGO is to destroy...to be the only voice."

"That's when things got real dicey," said Tru.

"The thoughts bought from EGO began to cause man all kinds of complications," said Percy. "People began to buy lies and gossip over truth. After a period of time, products of EGO began to create dis-ease in the body. People became sick and once-healthy bodies began to show signs of deterioration after years of buying impure, negative thoughts. Products such as revenge and resentment caused cancer, anger, and confusion caused healthy hearts to stop functioning. The thoughts of stress and anxiety were responsible for the general breakdown of the body. People had grown disconnected from one another. Thoughts sold by EGO were proving physically taxing to its consumers. Their thinking was literally killing them."

Uriah thought of the sick and lame who filled the streets of Kwo. Many of them appeared to have aged, well beyond their chronological years. They were often huddled in the corners, or beneath the awnings of the public dwellings, pleading for sustenance of any kind.

Uriah rarely saw the same people more than a few times. One day they would simply disappear, never to be seen again. Yet, as quickly as they vanished, they were replaced by another unfortunate soul. The weak and indigent on the streets of Kwo seemed to be in endless supply, like an assembly line of despair.

Percy told Uriah how the products of EGO had caused depression and acts of suicide. Thoughts of prejudice led to racism and division. Famine, poverty, and slavery were direct results from the purchase of thoughts, of absolute power and control. Thoughts of fear, judgment, and separation led to acts of terrorism, war and genocide. EGO had cornered the market on selling the population thoughts of negativity and unrest. It had become a world without love, beauty or imagination.

Uriah had been born into a world of thoughts run solely by the Company he had come to know now as EGO. Growing up, he saw the thought-police of this Company on every street corner.

They were men and woman who had accepted, even embraced, the Company control of their minds. Eventually these individuals became the willing subjects of EGO, doling out harsh punishment to those who refused to purchase the Company's products.

He had understood little of how the world had gotten this way, yet inside, he had always held the belief that there was hope for humanity, something greater for all. He felt inside that change was possible. Percy and Tru continued as best they could to fill in the background of how and why the world had reached this point.

"Soon acts of violence and small wars began to crop up across the globe," said Percy. "There was little the authorities and governments could do. Most became involved themselves."

"Course by that time, they was all pretty much affected by the thoughts sold by EGO too," added Tru.

"When any town or city would fall, EGO quickly and discreetly placed their own leaders in charge." Percy leaned forward in his chair, inching closer toward Uriah; his eyes had taken on a cold seriousness. "Soon all governing bodies became lifetime customers of EGO. It started on the local level until eventually all state and federal offices were replaced, and finally each country had succumbed to these thoughts. Its citizenry were subject to only those thoughts of EGO. The thought police of EGO controlled every town in an attempt to monitor the thoughts of the population. The people would consume the thoughts of EGO or suffer the consequences."

Uriah knew these police well. He had become adept at clearing his mind as he passed them on the street, making it difficult for them to read his thoughts. It was a skill his grandfather had taught him early on, and although he was only able to clear his mind for a few moments at a time, he was sure it had saved him from arrest more than once.

"Could thoughts cause all this to happen?" Uriah asked.

"Thoughts are never neutral, they are each very powerful," answered Percy. "Each thought alone carries a stream of energy which can either lift and empower or create chaos and despair. Imagine an entire planet of disempowering thoughts and ideas! Individually, these thoughts can be harmful, collectively they can be devastating. As thoughts are energy, this energy began to weigh heavily upon the world. The energy generated by these thoughts severely weakened the planet. It became thick and heavy like a quagmire of negativity. Before long, the earth was simply unable to handle the stress."

"That's when our resources started disappearin'," said Tru. "First the fresh water became infected and contaminated…"

"How did negative energy affect fresh water?" Uriah asked.

"The biochemical molecules of water are affected by thought and energy. The thoughts of EGO were everywhere, all the time. Destructive thinking began to affect all those things which feed our planet and sustain life. Fresh water was the most important. It is life's most perfect medium and it was destroyed by EGO."

"Seventy percent a' our bodies are made a' liquid ya' know?"

Uriah did not respond. He did not know about his body, being made of mostly water. All he knew of water was that in Kwo, it had to be boiled prior to drinking. Many people he knew became sick and died, as a result of not purifying the drinking water of bacteria and negative impurities. In several instances, people had gone mad from drinking unclean water.

"Then much of the plants and vegetation began to wilt and die for the same reason," continued Percy. "The soil itself had simply grown bad from the hateful energy. The earth was quickly losing its ability to support itself and humanity."

Uriah thought of Kwo and its lack of food supply. Most people in the town were starved, including him. And those who were not were severely lacking in nutrients and healthy sustenance. There was much hunger in Kwo. Fruits and vegetables were a luxury spoken of but never seen. Percy explained how the towns, such as Kwo and those like it had created a hybrid food source in order to feed its citizens. They were made to appear as fruits and vegetables, thus people believed they had been eating healthily grown plants.

"Thoughts affected the environment too," Tru added. "They was earthquakes, tornadas and lotsa' them hurricanes all over the planet, all a result of humanity's damagin' thoughts."

Uriah wondered to himself how thoughts could actually affect the weather, but chose to remain silent.

"Following on the heels of all this, the economy began to crumble and fall. And quite frankly it didn't take all too much to push it right over the edge," said Percy. "Once the food and water supply were diminished, people continued to fight with one another. They were all small skirmishes at first, neighbor against neighbor, friend against friend and then..." Percy paused a moment, he turned his palms up looking at Uriah as if he knew the conclusion.

"And then what?" asked Uriah eagerly.

"And then it led to the Great War of course," answered Percy, slightly puzzled.

A light bulb went off over Uriah's head, Percy and Tru saw it in his face immediately. "Yes," said Uriah remembering, "my grandfather told me stories of a tremendous battle which spread to every corner of the world. He said it destroyed much of mankind at the time."

"Your grandpa' was right a' course. At least sumptin' close ta' that," said Tru. "B'tween the disease, sickness and lack a' nutrient-rich food n' water, well folks started goin' mad and kept turnin' on one another right quick. War was what ya' might call inevitable."

"My grandfather told me it was a war of good against evil, but he wasn't sure about that. I have always believed he made that part up just for me," Uriah said, slightly embarrassed.

"I'm sure your grandfather believes that," Percy said, trying to let Uriah off the hook. "It is probably the way he remembers it. The real truth is there were no sides. No good, no evil; it was pretty much everyone for themselves. EGO sold thoughts of jealousy, envy and mistrust. They had infected the minds of man until there was no turning back. Eventually these thoughts of EGO caused man to turn on each other."

Uriah remembered again the stories of his grandfather. They were those of struggle and survival against overwhelming odds. He had been told many times how he was fortunate to be alive and that he should give thanks when he could do so safely. His grandfather never explained how this great battle between men had begun; he knew only the side he and Uriah supported in their hearts had been defeated. The thoughts of the Company had prevailed over those of God.

"That's how the thoughts of EGO work," continued Percy. "They were like a disease of the mind causing one man to be suspicious and afraid of the next. People grew steadily angrier with each other and with themselves. The small battles and pockets of confrontations grew steadily, eventually leading to the war. By the time anyone noticed what was happening, it had become a full-scale global conflict and mankind stood on the brink of elimination."

"Weren't anything to do then but pray," said Tru, shaking his head.

"Unfortunately, not enough people realized that prayer was exactly the remedy for our troubles," said Percy, with heavy resignation.

"Why didn't they see it then?" asked Uriah. He spoke like a young idealist, which made Percy and Tru smile.

"They just wasn't in that mind to do so," added Tru. "Folks had forgotten all about buying thoughts from the Source." Tru shook his head in dismay. "No sir, EGO wouldn't allow it anyways. They had infected mans' mind something awful by then."

"So, what were they fighting for?" asked Uriah. It was a part of the story his grandfather could never fill.

"All that negative thinking caused man to turn on one another."

"You believe that?" asked Uriah, still slightly skeptical.

"I sure do, part of it anyway. If every man was his own army of sorts, there was no unity. It was a free for all kind of chaos. No objective, no goals, no mission of any kind, simply diseased thoughts causing us to turn on each other. As far as I'm concerned it was nothing more than that. As the world weakened, EGO grew stronger until they ultimately took control. As I said, the thought-police employed by EGO took over and began popping up on every corner in every town. After some time the world just settled into an uneasy form of peace."

"An uneasy peace?"

"Well people got tired of fighting and simply accepted their lot in life. They weren't happy, but they just kind of slipped into a pattern and went along."

"Not all folks was perfectly happy b'fore, but at least the choice to buy the thoughts a' God was available," added Tru.

"People have been living this miserable type of existence ever since and it's just the way EGO wants it," Percy began again. "No dreams or lofty pursuits, nothing to inspire mankind toward betterment in any way. No love or compassion for our fellow man. No thoughts or inclinations to grow and propel man into the future, just bleak day-to-day thoughts of survival. The thoughts sold by EGO will keep man there indefinitely," Percy said.

Uriah understood this existence well. He had seen many of his townspeople trudge through a bleak and unforgiving existence of debilitating thoughts.

He was certain, if he had always felt unhappy with being forced to purchase the thoughts of EGO; certainly there must be others. But he also believed most were afraid of the change that he always knew was possible. To Uriah, his belief in something more outweighed his fear of the Company. He wished others could take the risk, rather than slowly wither in misery.

Uriah sat quietly for a moment and then thought back to what Percy had said and asked, "How do you know all this?" He was embarrassed and hoped Percy didn't suspect him of disbelieving his story. If Percy took offense, he hid it well.

Percy did not answer right away. He looked out the window at a new day of sunshine and took a deep breath, "Well," he said turning to Uriah," my grandfather used to tell me stories too, "he smiled.

□■ TWELVE ■□

More than two months had passed since arriving in Hope, and Uriah had settled in well. He had chosen to remain with Tru, until a dwelling of his own had been built.

Although his time was his to do with as he pleased, he had fallen into a semi-routine of growth and learning at the tutelage of Percy and Tru. He learned more of the Great War and the misery which followed. He learned more about the strong hold the company of EGO had on its people. Percy also taught him the history of Hope: How it had become a place for refugees who understood the power of thoughts sold only by God; a place for minds to purchase the thoughts they chose.

"I knew you was to belong here when I saw ya' straight away," said Tru. Uriah felt honored Tru saw this in him.

He learned about how the war had come to an end sometime late in the year 2175. Although, Percy would add, the war for control of man's thoughts has never truly ended.

"It continues to this day," he told Uriah. "For EGO, the war won't be over until every last man on earth has stopped buying his thoughts from God."

Uriah was told that Company-owned villages and walled communities had not been the typical living conditions in the past. Percy explained how many people had been free to live where they chose and to come and go as they pleased from city to town. Restricted living conditions were a result of the war and the society left in its wake. And this was how EGO was able to isolate and separate the population.

"Industry was destroyed, and most cities of the world were reduced to rubble," Percy told him. "Any technology that was left was used for purposes of control by EGO. Hope had become the last remaining bastion on earth where people were free to buy thoughts from the Source. EGO would love nothing more than to infect and destroy it as well."

His talks with Percy and Tru validated much of what he had always believed deep in his heart—a belief that he could create the destiny of his dreams, if only he were committed to believing so. The products of God were available here. In Hope, he was free to purchase only those thoughts which brought him closer to his destiny. For Uriah, it was a matter of what that destiny was which plagued him. He wanted a life with Akuna, this he knew without question. He wanted the freedom to pursue those things which his heart desired. Yet, something was absent, a calling, perhaps. If only he knew what it was, he would gladly pay God his due and follow that calling. He prayed often for his destiny to be revealed. And he gave thanks for an answer, although it had yet to be provided. As each day passed, without an answer, his faith in God did not diminish, but grew stronger. Such was the benefit of life in Hope.

When he wasn't listening to Percy and Tru, Uriah took advantage of the variety of activities offered him in Hope, experiencing life as he never had before. Fishing, gardening, and reading from Percy's book collection filled much of his time. He wrote in his journal daily and openly, an act he had risked a great deal while in Kwo. Mostly, he wrote of his thoughts surrounding Akuna and his feelings for her. He did not need to question whether she was happy, he knew of no one in the town of Kwo who was permitted such thoughts. Although he was happy and he knew Akuna was not, Uriah did not buy the guilt of EGO Tru had warned him about. He knew if he had any hope of rescuing Akuna, he would have to be on solid ground with his thoughts. Thoughts of guilt and remorse no longer had a place in Uriah's heart or mind. Regarding Akuna, his thoughts were purchased solely from the Source, and he willingly paid the price.

Uriah's knowledge of life outside the walls of Kwo had expanded with each passing day. He planted his own garden and tended to it regularly. In Kwo, he had worked as a stone laborer for the Company, like so many of his neighbors. He was charged to reinforce the walls of Kwo, which seemed in constant need of repair. Most did not realize the walls were designed to hold the people in, as much as keep the wanderers out. He knew little of cultivation and farming, but his love for growing his own food had already produced amazing results. Fruits and vegetables had become a staple of his diet, as it had for all citizens in Hope, and he was eager to create a vibrant garden and contribute to the food supply in his new home. In Kwo, the residents were told that the soil would not produce food. They were told that the land had been destroyed and was barren of all nutrients, and the seeds that remained from the War had grown old and stale.

"Bad seeds planted in rotting soil made for bad results," the people were told. There was no longer any use in trying.

One day Uriah asked Tru how it was possible to grow such abundant and delicious vegetation in Hope.

"Godly soil son," he answered briskly. "That an' a belief it's possible. 'Member what we tole ya', fertile mind and fertile seeds equals fertile results." Uriah became convinced that, as his vegetable garden grew, so grew the garden of his mind.

Tru also loved to fish. It was an experience he had shared with his son many times. On some days, Uriah would join him, and Tru enjoyed passing on his skills as an angler to the young man. He taught him to bait a hook and reel in a catch, but mostly the two men talked. That was the real joy for Uriah and also for Tru.

One day the two men were enjoying a lazy morning along the bank of a small lake. The location was a favorite of Tru's, which he had discovered years earlier. It was a spot where he had had great luck in catching fish. At this spot, trout, bass and others always seemed to find Tru's hook with ease.

Their lines had been in the water for barely a minute when Uriah turned to his fishing mate, "Tru, do you mind if I ask you about your son?" he began nervously.

Tru looked at him and smiled, putting the young man immediately at ease, "Ask away."

"What's his name?"

"Deel. My boy's name is Deel," said Tru. "He's about yer age, maybe a little older. Good looking feller like his pop," he laughed.

"The first day I was in Hope you said you pray he comes back. Where is he now?"

Tru shrugged his shoulders and his face became scrunched, "Not sure," he said shaking his head slowly. "Been gone 'bout five years now and ain't heard from in that time."

Uriah opened his mouth to speak, when Tru raised his hand stifling his questions. "No need son, I'll spill 'em. Talkin' always helps, I figure. See, Deel and I come to Hope 'bout six years or so ago. Deel's mother passed when he was just a boy. Some kinda' sickness we couldn't figure took her fast 'fore anyone could do a thing." Tru stared off in the distance as he spoke. To Uriah, he looked as though he was reliving the experience of losing his wife, and he instantly regretted asking him about his family. "If ya' ask me, I think she jus' gave up. Folks can do that when they're unhappy."

He went on to explain how he and Deel had come to Hope after leaving his town. According to Tru the two had left like "thieves in the night." The way the big man described his town, Uriah thought it sounded very much like Kwo. The people were forced to buy the poverty, the misery, and the thoughts of EGO. Just as in Kwo, the thought police, too, stood on every corner in his town.

"Sumptin' in here," said Tru, pointing to his heart. "Sumptin' tole' me there was more to life than that place. Jus' like you," he smiled. "I knew happiness, whatever that was, was not in that place. I needed a place that let me think as my heart wanted, even if I weren't sure where exactly that place was." Tru looked up at the clouds passing slowly overhead. The sky behind them was a brilliant azure blue. "This place," said Tru, "jus' seems to call to some folks. Folks like me an' you."

Tru sighed deeply and continued, not missing a beat, "After my wife died, I didn't want to suffer the same fate and leave Deel all alone in the world, such as it was, a' course. We was all each other had. And once Percy took us in, well then we both had Hope."

Tru told Uriah how, initially, things had been great in Hope. He and Deel were encouraged to buy their thoughts from the Source. Happiness, dreams, and inspiration were available and possible to Tru and his son, for the first time in their lives. And then suddenly, his son seemed to stop believing in the power of the Source. "He jus' didn't seem to take to the thoughts a' God anymore, almost like he didn't deserve it in his heart."

"What happened?" asked Uriah. His voice had risen to match his level of concern.

"Don't get nervous son, you'll scare the fish," said Tru laughing, but his smile quickly faded, when he brought the subject back to his son. "Fact is, EGO caught hold of 'em." Tru shook his head again slowly, staring at the point where his line disappeared into the water.

"Yup," he said, never taking his eyes off the line. "He bought the doubt, the fear, and the insecurity."

"Even here in Hope?" asked Uriah.

Tru chuckled, "Sure, EGO never let's ya' go. They'll follo' ya' everywhere. They'll sell ya' on the notion you're always needin' more. Deel sure did believe that and they knew it. That's how they got my boy, I'm sure of it. He jus' believed he weren't enough. One day he bought some greed and inadequacy and left Hope in search a' more..."

Tru looked at Uriah and frowned. "More a' what is what I can't figure. Anyways, I noticed he got might edgy leadin' up to his leavin' here, started getting kinda' antsy, unhappy like. Sorta' like he weren't quite sure what to do with the peace and fulfilling life Hope was a' offerin.'" Uriah watched Tru as he looked out over the lake; Tru's stare now a thousand miles away.

"The ole man and I tried to work with 'em. But it ain't like in those EGO-run towns. Ya' can't force folks to buy thoughts here in Hope. Training yourself to buy the thoughts that serve you takes a might bit a' work, he jus' weren't used to it. And I guess he just weren't ready to either."

Tru leaned his head back and stared at the sky. "Seems no matter how hard ya' try, some folks get used to bein' miserable and unhappy, like they's comfortable in pain an' there ain't no talkin' 'em out of it. They never look to change them ways and they stay stuck like that for life."

Tru again looked out over the lake, suddenly he smiled and turned to Uriah "Ain't no sense in me buyin' the sorrow, though, is there? You jus' keep feeding that good wolf son, an' you'll be alright."

Uriah wasn't sure what Tru meant by feeding the good wolf. Was there a test which required him to feed a ferocious yet apparently friendly wolf? Was this a reference to Deel? Uriah didn't want to keep Tru talking along the subject of his son any longer, yet his curiosity got the better of him. "What do you mean by feeding the good wolf?" he asked.

Tru chuckled and proceeded to tell Uriah an old Native American legend. It was the story of an aging Cherokee warrior attempting to teach his grandson about life. The old man told the boy how inside him were two wolves. One was evil. It was filled with hate, anger, violence, resentment regret, self pity, and arrogance. The other wolf was good. It was filled with love, compassion, hope, serenity, kindness, empathy, and generosity. This fight was going on inside of every person who lives, he told the boy. The wolves fought, explained the grandfather, for the dominance of the souls of all who lived. When the boy asked his grandfather which wolf will win the fight going on inside him, the grandfather replied. "The one who will win is the one you feed the most."

Uriah thought about this story a moment. He wondered, too, if Tru had shared this legend with his son. He guessed at some point he had.

"How do we feed the good wolf?" asked Uriah, suspecting he already knew the answer.

"A steady diet a' buyin' thoughts a' the Source, oughta' do it," answered Tru proudly.

"I know you been told this already, but it bears repeatin', agin' and agin,' if ya' ask me," said Tru. "Thoughts is right powerful forms a' energy, maybe the most in the entire universe. They create the seen from the unseen; make the possible from the impossible. But they can also be destructive. They can destroy a life, a family, a community, a nation, heck even a planet," as he waved his arm across the lake. "Most folks are unaware, but these here thoughts are the guidin' force of their life. Them choices ya' make, them ones ya' put most your energy upon, them are the ones that 'ell bear ya' fruit, for good or fer bad."

Uriah leaned back against a large tree behind him. His fishing pole lay unattended on the ground to his right. "Feed the good wolf," he said, nodding almost to himself and Tru smiled.

To Uriah, the day was perfect. A light breeze blew in from behind them, cooling their necks and brought the sweet fragrance of summer. They were known as easterlies, according to Percy. He said these winds brought with them the gift of God's wisdom.

The two men sat in silence for the next several minutes. Each man bought thoughts of gratitude for the peaceful and serene moment they shared in nature. Silence was one of the many benefits in Hope. This was a place where a man could shut off his thoughts and, if he chose, bask in the serenity of nothingness. Uriah had yet to learn how to best use this luxury.

Finally, it was Uriah who broke the silence. "Do you ever think to look for Deel?" He immediately wanted to take back the question, but Tru did not appear bothered by it.

"I did a' course, searched far and wide, town to town. Near got grabbed a few times ma'self. Not sure where to look tho' anymore, and I know he'll come back when it's right. Also, I figured the best way to help the world was from right here in Hope. Right here is where we keep the thoughts a' the Source from fadin' away." Tru let out a half hearted laugh, which Uriah thought sounded forced. "Right here is where we keep hope alive, ya' might say. When the thoughts a' God are alive, there'll always be Hope."

"Is it hard not knowing?" asked Uriah boldly.

Tru nodded, "It 'tis at that." Again, he did not appear bothered by his questions.

"Mind if I ask you a question?" said Tru. Uriah shook his head, "No, go ahead.

"Why did you leave Akuna behind?" His question was soft, but direct.

"I wanted her to come," answered Uriah hesitantly. "But it wasn't my choice. Now I don't believe I'll ever see her again."

"There's always a choice," snapped Tru. "Stop buying those thoughts a' EGO tellin' ya' you ain't got no control. Fact is ya'; knew the only way to help her was to help yourself first. Ya' had to get yourself happy first. Otherwise, you're no good to anyone. Ya' find ya' jus' keep draggin' each another down all the time. There's two things I learned since comin' here ta' Hope. The first is the thoughts a' EGO are everywhere, jus' like the thoughts a God. Second, ya' can't convince others to buy the thoughts you think they ought to be buyin,' because it's always their choice."

Tru paused for a moment and tilted his head back. He took in a deep, full breath through his considerably sized nose and closed his eyes, allowing the sun full on his face. Then he said softly, "Though I do believe one day Deel will return. Yup, I continue to buy the faith that he will indeed return one day. I know in my bones he will. And you'd best be served to have the same faith you'll be with this Akuna person again. If ya' really want somethin' in life, ya' must align your thoughts with what it is you desire. Thoughts from God is the only way. If ya' don't believe, ya' don't get."

Tru's words caused Uriah to pause. It was in this moment he decided he would return for Akuna and his grandfather and convince them to join him in Hope.

"I got me one!" Tru shouted, startling Uriah back to the present. Tru's line suddenly went taut and after a brief struggle of man against fish, Tru's angling skills proved victorious as he reeled in a plump, hearty lake trout.

"Congratulations," said Uriah. "I haven't got as much as a nibble."

"It's gonna' be hard to reel in a fish when your not holdin' the pole," laughed Tru, holding his substantial catch up to admire. "Ya' gotta' take some action, after all."

Uriah quickly picked up the pole. He remembered the most important element Tru had taught him about fishing: Give thanks and gratitude for the opportunity to fish.

He would purchase the patience and knowingness that God would provide a catch. He paid the asking price of taking action, and again, offered thanks for the opportunity. He held the pole firmly in his hands with expectancy, and within seconds his line went taut.

□■ THIRTEEN ■□

Despite the protests of Percy and Tru, Uriah continued preparations for his trip back to Kwo. He would go and bring back his grandfather and Akuna. He knew it would be difficult, but his mission was one of purpose and intent.

"Be sure to seek the signs of God," advised Percy. "They are everywhere, but you must acknowledge them. Remember, there is never a time He is not speaking to you and offering His services."

Percy knew that a man of intention was an undeniable force. Uriah was armed with faith and a newfound destiny: a destiny to save Akuna from a life of doubt, hardship, and fear. He would save her from a lifetime in Kwo, a lifetime with no possibility of happiness and only the thoughts of EGO to fill her mind.

There was also the matter of his grandfather. Uriah knew his grandfather would claim himself too old to travel. While it was true he was indeed set in his ways, often telling Uriah that old habits were hard to break, even the ones that do not serve us, Uriah held a strong faith that he could convince him to return to Hope anyway. He believed he could convince his grandfather' that his own stories were true, and he would realize the magical place he spoke of was not a legend, but a beautiful reality. Uriah bought the faith that he could convince them both to leave Kwo to join him in Hope, a place where they would have the opportunity to choose the thoughts of God.

His journey back to Kwo would not be easy. During his exodus to Hope, he had been able to follow the stars as his grandfather had suggested. He would have no such luxury this time. This time the stars which led him would be at his back. He would be forced to retrace his steps to Kwo from memory and instinct. But he did have something else, something he did not have on his journey to Hope, Uriah was armed with an overwhelming belief he would succeed.

"If you must go," Percy told him, "be sure to keep a generous serving of faith with you at all times. It will guide you and keep you strong when things look bleak. Allow it to lead you, should you become lost."

Uriah agreed. He packed his backpack with fruits, breads and as much water as he could carry. He spent that evening in prayer, buying only those thoughts of the Source, arming himself with love, faith, humility and compassion.

The words of Tru echoed in his head and he prepared himself against the enemy to his mind.

"You must be careful," he told Uriah. "EGO is patient and clever 'an they'll do their darndest to sell ya' on thoughts a' doubt and fear. They'll peck at yer mind like a buzzard. They'll try to weaken ya' 'til ya' give in."

Then Tru said something which made Uriah turn cold, "Or worse, they'll make ya' one a' theirs again, iffen they can. You jus' keep buyin' the faith from God an' you'll be alright."

Uriah gave thanks and lay down for the night of rest. He would leave at first light. The next morning, as he left the town limits, Uriah spotted a sign he had not seen when he had entered Hope months earlier. The sign read, "You are now leaving Hope. Feel free to take some with you on your travels." Uriah nodded, "Must be Tru's doing," he thought to himself, smiling as he continued walking.

By late afternoon on the first day, Uriah had reached the top of the hill where he had first spotted Hope more than a month earlier. He was able to navigate the field of tall grass much easier this time. It was as if the field of reeds had cleared in conjunction with his field of thoughts. "I am seeing things much clearer now," he thought to himself. My obstacles have become worn, trodden paths of determination and focus.

That evening he made camp again on the ridge beneath the two large oaks. From his position, he could clearly see the lights of Hope, now that he knew where to look. We are only able to see something when we are certain it exists, yet true faith is in believing in those things we do not see, he thought to himself.

It was surreal, thought Uriah. He had risked his life to reach a magical place he did not know existed, and now he was leaving that place to return to the one filled with hardship and misery, from which he had been cast out only months ago. He knew if he were discovered in Kwo, he would be thrown in jail immediately, or worse.

As he traveled, Uriah again, kept close to the tree line as much as possible, hoping to remain out of sight of any bandits. He was cautious to stay quiet and kept vigilant for any signs of potential danger. He prayed frequently, asking God for guidance and signs that he might find his way back to Kwo. His path was rockier than he remembered, and he prayed, too, for the strength to endure.

Uriah seemed to sense something, in each new town he neared, that he could not accurately describe. There was heaviness and the people he saw held a zombie-like sadness on their faces not present in Hope. These towns and their people appeared void of energy and life. This energy of sadness had become more apparent to Uriah, after his time spent in Hope.

Occasionally, he attempted to transmit his thoughts to Akuna, regarding his impending arrival, sending forth those thoughts and feelings of love. His faith was his only evidence that his thoughts could reach her.

On the morning of the fourth day, Uriah had reached a town he remembered immediately. It was a place where he had visited on his way to Hope. He was thankful Percy and Tru had given him goods, for which to trade for food and water, and was relieved for any opportunities to unload a few pounds from his pack.

As Uriah entered the town, he was careful not to think those thoughts that might arouse suspicion with the local police. He chose to clear his mind of thought. He had become adept at this skill, managing to fool the authorities on several occasions. He thanked his grandfather for teaching him this art and continued farther into the city limits.

He was able to exchange writing tablets, drawings, and in one instance, a small quartz stone he had found in Hope for some bread and water. He purchased blessings from the Source to purify his food. Although the bread was stale and the water was murky, unlike in Hope, he remained grateful, always remembering to give thanks to God for his bounty. At night, he prayed for the ability to see himself as God saw him: a man of faith, deserving of His offerings.

When Uriah was sure it was safe, he again told the townspeople of the thoughts offered by the Source. He spoke of Hope and the possibilities that existed for them there. Just as before, many refused to believe him or were too afraid to listen.

Before Uriah left this town, he was approached by an old man. The man had overheard others talking about a stranger who told stories on thoughts sold by God. Uriah's stories of Hope and the Source were beginning to spread and he grew afraid he would be arrested if he did not leave soon.

"Are you the young man who talks about a mythical place where the thoughts of God are available?" the old man asked Uriah in a whisper.

Uriah was hesitant to respond. He feared this may be a trap arranged by the Company. but his reliance on faith kept him strong. "Yes I am," he nodded. "And it is not a mythical place. Do you know of Hope?"

"When I was a boy," said the old man, "I heard stories of a place not far from here. It was near the sea under the brightest stars. It was a place of the possibilities of God, a place where a man could be all he could dream to be in life, a place where man was limited only by his own imagination."

A slight smile crept across the old man's face and Uriah could see his eyes begin to sparkle. "I have not heard these stories for many years. I have always believed in my heart that there was such a place."

The old man asked Uriah to tell him the stories of Hope. He said there were others who had heard of this place as well. "Many of the old people in this town have heard the stories of this land, but they are afraid to believe in the possibilities offered there."

The old man shook his head in resignation and continued. "Most of the younger generation is unaware that such a place exists. The Company has imprisoned or sent away many who speak of this place. But I am very old and no longer fear the punishment of the Company."

Uriah told the old man why he was returning to Kwo. He confirmed the stories he had heard of Hope were indeed true. It was a place where the thoughts and ideas of God were available to all who were willing to pay the price. If they would do this simple gesture, then all things were possible to all who sought His product.

Uriah promised he would return for the man and take him to Hope, once he had found Akuna and his grandfather. "I can take you there," he told the man. To Uriah's surprise, the old man adamantly refused. "I am tired and too old to change my thoughts and too set in my ways. I have lived in misery and poverty because of the thoughts I am forced to buy. I will die having never experienced the thoughts of God. But I have a favor to ask of you. I can see there is good in your heart and so I ask, when you return to Hope, would you take my granddaughter with you? She lives there in the dwelling at the base of the hill," he said as he pointed to a modest straw roofed shack.

"She will protest, I know," continued the old man, "but you must convince her. Her name is Natta and I want her to live a life of dreams and happiness. Promise me you will do that for me."

Uriah agreed. He tried again to have the old man agree to journey back to Hope with him when he returned. But in spite of Uriah's assurances, the old man again refused and turned and walked away, disappearing into the streets.

More than a week later, Uriah was able to reach the walls of Kwo, the oldest and largest EGO-run city. Because of this, Kwo was also one of the few walled cities in the region, and it was heavily guarded, unlike many towns owned by the Company. It would prove difficult to enter, yet Uriah had a plan. He knew of a secret entrance he had discovered when he was a stoneworker reinforcing the wall. Although he disliked his job, which pleased the Company immensely, his knowledge of the stone fortifications was now proving to be a blessing in disguise.

It was already late in the day when Uriah arrived outside of Kwo. He would rest for a few hours until nightfall and he would sneak into the city under the cover of darkness. He understood the consequences, if he were discovered. But it was a risk he was more than willing to take to rescue Akuna and his grandfather.

Uriah awoke a few hours later to a moonless night. God, he felt, was on his side. He entered the city easily and began the two mile walk through the streets of Kwo to reach Akuna. He kept his head down and his pace brisk to lower his chances of being recognized. He was confident the thought-police would hardly notice him, as long as he was able to fully clear his mind of Godly thoughts. Within an hour, he was at Akuna's window, arriving undetected. He was overjoyed to find her awake and alone. But when she saw him, it was not the greeting Uriah had hoped for.

"What are you doing here, Uriah?" she asked in a panic. "If they find you here, the Company will surely kill you."

"Akuna, I am so glad to see you!" began Uriah, excitedly. "My grandfather's stories were true! I have traveled the wilderness for many miles to find you. There is a place, a town called Hope. It is filled with the thoughts of God. It is free from the oppression of the Company. The thoughts of God are available to us there."

Uriah told Akuna how he had come for her. He wanted her to return to Hope with him. They could be married and live a life filled with dreams and possibilities. Together they could live any destiny they chose.

"I love you, Akuna," he said.

"Please don't say that, Uriah," she pleaded.

"I have never been able to express my love before, Akuna," he continued, ignoring her protestations. "I have always loved you. I want you to return with me and become my wife." But Uriah underestimated the power EGO held over the thoughts of the people, especially Akuna. She was filled with too much fear of the Company.

"You must not talk like that" she cried. "You know love is not allowed here. They will read your thoughts and they will come for you."

"That is why we must leave right away," he assured her.

He did his best to convince Akuna to leave with him, but she refused to believe. She did not own the trust, and her fear was too much for him to overcome. She had bought only doubt and fear in her life and held no concept of happiness. But Uriah had another plan, one which involved his grandfather.

"You must talk to my grandfather," he pleaded. "He will tell you about this place, just as I have. His stories of Hope are what convinced me to find it. He will tell y-"

Akuna's face grew grim, causing Uriah to stop abruptly. His heart began to race as a feeling of dread washed over him. "What is it, Akuna? Why do you look so sad?"

"Uriah," she whispered softly with tears in her eyes. "Your grandfather, he was imprisoned by the Company."

"What? When?"

"One week ago," she sobbed. "He was caught talking to a man about a place where the thoughts of God existed. He talked with this man about the stories, just as he did with you."

"What man? Who?"

"I don't know," she cried. "He was a stranger. The two spoke openly about the thoughts of God, but your grandfather was arrested. This man, I believe he got away."

"I must get him out of prison," Uriah said, defiantly pounding his fist in his hand.

"You don't understand," she continued, her gaze falling at his feet. "He died there yesterday. He was deeply saddened when you were forced to leave Kwo. He missed you very much. But he secretly prayed for you to discover the place beneath the stars. He prayed it was real. He would have been pleased to know that it was."

Uriah looked at Akuna, his mouth hung open in shock. "He was very old, Uriah," she continued.

"When I went to visit him, he told me that he believed in his heart you had found happiness and you were safe. It was a feeling he had, I think he called this feeling a faith? He said he believed he could die happy believing you were well. I feel he was happy in the end, even though the Company tried to stop his thoughts of happiness."

Uriah was saddened by the loss of his grandfather, but knew he was running out of time in Kwo.

"Why won't you come with me then, Akuna?" Tears were beginning to form in his eyes. "My grandfather was right, and we can be together there."

"Misery and sadness are all I know," she sobbed. "I am not happy, but no one here is, and I have grown accustomed to the thoughts of the Company. My mind and heart are too filled with fear and doubt to risk change."

"But a happy life is waiting for you," said Uriah desperately. "A life where the choice to think the thoughts of God are possible."

"I'm sorry," whispered Akuna, gently stroking his cheek. "A life of happiness and the thoughts of God, as you say, are foreign to me. The fear of the life you say is possible for me is more terrifying than the unhappiness I am forced to buy from the Company. "Please," she said turning away, "you must go now, before you are caught."

Uriah went silent, as a heavy blanket of mourning fell over him. He had not felt this level of sadness since living in Kwo. Anger and confusion began to swirl in his head. He had bought faith and a belief from the Source, and now he felt he had been betrayed by God. He left Hope and braved the wild with a faith that he would return with them both. Now his grandfather was dead and Akuna was filled with too much fear to leave her home of misery. Without uttering another plea, Uriah left Akuna and began walking back through the streets of Kwo. He made no attempt to mask his thoughts, as he passed the police on the street. If they were to enter his mind, they would find him depressed, betrayed, and miserable, a loyal customer of EGO, and they would be pleased.

Uriah slipped back through the wall out of Kwo. He felt lost, unsure where to go and he was no longer inspired to return to Hope. In his present state, he would do nothing more than wander the wilderness, like the bandits and the lost souls in his grandfather's stories. He would make no attempt to hide from strangers or potential danger, leaving him exposed and open to predators.

He wandered through that night and into the next day without direction or purpose. By noon of the third day, the sun was high upon him, and the heat made it difficult for him to think. Since leaving Kwo, he had gone without food, sleep, or water. His grandfather and Akuna were lost to him forever, as was all interest in returning to Hope. He soon became weary and sick and suddenly Uriah dropped to the ground, passing out in an open field.

While he lay there unconscious, Uriah had a dream. In his dream, he was beneath a flowing waterfall, his mouth was open trying to drink from the rushing water, but the water tasted metallic and was filled with dirt. He tried to filter the water with his cracked, dry lips, but only a few drops found their way to the back of his parched throat. No matter how much the waterfall offered, he could not get enough to quench his thirst.

"Drink...drink...drink," came a soft voice. Uriah tried to heed the ghostly commands and gulped at the water. In his dream, he could feel a very real heavenly feeling of liquid coating his barren throat.

"Drink," repeated the voice, more clearly this time.

Uriah now realized he was no longer in a dream state. He blinked his eyes several times in an attempt to wake and right his vision. The sun directly above him made this task difficult.

"Are you alright?" came the unfamiliar voice.

Uriah opened his eyes fully now. A man was kneeling over him holding his head. He held a rusted can of water to Uriah's lips, urging him to drink slowly.

"Are you alright?" repeated the man.

Uriah tried to speak, but opted instead, for another drink of water.

"Why are you lying here in the open?" asked the stranger.

Uriah struggled to sit upright, but was unsuccessful. The man helped to prop him up to a seated position.

"I, I mus' have pass'd out from the heat," he mumbled, nearly incoherent.

"I was wandering…," said Uriah, before his words trailed off becoming inaudible. The stranger slowly poured more water past his lips.

"Are you alone?" queried the stranger, scanning the horizon. Uriah nodded and continued to drink.

"Can you stand?" Uriah nodded again. "We need to get you out of the sun." Uriah was too weak to protest anyway, and the stranger helped him to his feet, bracing him at the waist.

"There is a small patch of brush over there," the man said, motioning behind Uriah. "There is some shade where you can rest a while."

The two men headed for the shade of the brush. Uriah's legs were weak and he needed the stranger's aid to walk.

"Thank you for your help," Uriah said feebly.

"You are welcome. I'm glad I came along when I did. It is very dangerous out here alone. I've been told that there are many wild animals and even wilder humans."

"My name is Uriah," he said weakly.

"It is nice to meet you, Uriah," said the stranger smiling. "My name is Deel."

□■ FOURTEEN ■□

Uriah had rested in this place overnight. When he awoke, he was surprised to see his new friend was still with him, and he was feeling strong enough to travel.

Deel and Uriah had been walking for a few hours. There was safety in togetherness, Uriah thought. He had told Deel about meeting his father in Hope and how he prayed for his safe return. He told him Tru seemed well, but he felt concern for his son. With each step he took, Uriah's heart grew heavier over the loss of his grandfather and the absence of Akuna.

Finally, Uriah asked, "Why did you leave Hope?"

"I'm not sure I can say for certain. I tried to find my way back, up here," answered Deel, pointing to his head. "But I was lost, because thoughts of the head are not the way to find yourself, it has to come from the heart. As best as I can remember, things were great in Hope. I was happy and my life was full of possibilities. Then one day, I began to take God's gifts for granted. I started to believe I was the source of any success or happiness in my life and I stopped trusting in the thoughts of God."

Uriah then told Deel the story of how he had come to find Hope, after being banished from his home of Kwo. "I traveled in the direction of the sea, following the setting sun, and at night the brightest star," said Uriah.

"How did you know to do that?" Deel asked. He was impressed a young man alone could make such a journey without a true direction.

"My grandfather told me stories about a place that sold the thoughts of God."

"Had he been there before?" asked Deel.

"No," said Uriah regretfully. "He had never been out of Kwo in his life."

"Then how did he know of Hope?"

"Someone had told him stories of it," answered Uriah.

"But they were just stories," said Deel, puzzled. "What would you do if your grandfather had been wrong and Hope did not exist or was somewhere else?"

"I dunno," said Uriah, shrugging his shoulders. "I tried not to think about that too much. I focused on grandfather's words and had faith it would be there. He told me to always have a faith and belief in possibilities." Uriah paused a moment, then said, "Your dad told me that too."

Deel nodded, but remained silent.

A thought suddenly struck Deel. Deel said he had been in Kwo, for the same reason Uriah had visited so many of the towns dotted along the landscape. Although it was extremely risky for any stranger entering these communities, supplies were needed. Deel had little with which to trade, mostly he begged for handouts and stole whatever food he could, coming within mere moments of being arrested on several occasions. He was ashamed for taking what was not his, but he had to survive, he reasoned. Deel had been miserable and Kwo was simply another town of many.

He realized that the old man he had been speaking with in Kwo, when they were ambushed by the thought police, was more than likely, Uriah's grandfather.

"I believe I spoke with him," said Deel tentatively.

"Who?"

"Your grandfather," Deel answered tentatively. "He was arrested for speaking about the thoughts of God. He spoke about his grandson, but never referred to you by name. Perhaps it was to protect you. He told me he felt in his heart that you were well. He missed you a great deal."

"You spoke with my grandfather?!" asked Uriah, excitedly. "What happened? Where you there when he was taken?"

He told Uriah how his grandfather had been arrested and he assumed thrown in prison by the thought police. Deel had been fortunate enough to escape.

"That is when I left Kwo," Deel said. "We had talked about Hope and of you. Your grandfather was good to me," continued Deel. "He gave me food and water and offered me a place to sleep, when no one else would. Most were too afraid to show compassion or empathy for fear of the thought police. In spite of the dangers, your grandfather showed me kindness."

Deel stopped abruptly, looking directly into Uriah's eyes. "Your grandfather's actions are what convinced me to return to Hope. It is why I didn't rob you back in the field where I found you. If he could show kindness to a stranger, at the risk to his safety, then I could as well. I decided then, after meeting your grandfather that I would seek to help others. That is when they came for us, but he was old and did not get away. I feel...," said Deel, his tone fell soft and sheepish, "I feel I may have gotten him arrested."

Uriah did not blame Deel, and he let him know it. "My grandfather often spoke of happiness and of leaving Kwo, but he would not leave me. The Company watched him closely. It was not your fault. He knew the risks of speaking on the thoughts of God. It was his way of helping others. I wanted my grandfather to see Hope," he said sadly. "I so badly wanted him to see that his stories were true."

Deel tried to lift Uriah's spirits, which he could see were falling fast. "Maybe there is a way we can save him," said Deel.

Tears began welling in the corners of Uriah's eyes. "He died a few days ago," he sobbed. "He died in prison, before I was able to see him."

'I'm sorry," said Deel, growing uncomfortable. "You know," he added trying to comfort his friend, "maybe he can see Hope through you."

"Maybe he can," said Uriah, forcing a smile.

"I am certain your grandfather loved you very much," said Deel, compassionately. Uriah nodded, he knew that as well. Although it was illegal to express love of any kind in Kwo, he had always sensed it from his grandfather. Love was the number one product of the Source, and the mere thought of it brought swift and unyielding punishment from the Company. Still, the authorities could not prevent those feelings in one's heart.

"If it had not been for your grandfather, I would not be returning to Hope. He made me realize how important it is to share the thoughts of God with others. And also how important it is to be with our loved ones." Deel looked up at the sky and smiled. "Your grandfather made me realize how much I miss my father and his teachings." Uriah smiled inside, for a moment…he felt like he was talking to Tru. Yes, thought Uriah, he is definitely Tru's son.

The two men walked in silence for awhile. Neither had spoken openly about the direction each chose to follow, although they walked toward Hope. Uriah, still in a state of mourning over the loss of his grandfather and the absence of Akuna, had no specific course. His intention was to wander, yet he sorely needed companionship, and someone to talk to. Without realizing, he followed whatever direction Deel was headed.

They continued to walk in silence for a long time until Deel finally spoke, "Why did you leave Hope and return to Kwo?" Immediately he regretted asking, for fear it would again bring up thoughts of his grandfather, but before he could retract his question and change the subject, Uriah answered.

"For my grandfather…" Uriah said solemnly, "and for a girl. But she refused to come with me. She is too filled with fear and doubt."

"Do you love her?"

"Yes very much."

"Does she love you?"

"I believed she did. As you know the expression of love is not allowed in Kwo, but…" Uriah shook his head in frustration, "now I am not so certain if she ever loved me at all."

"Is she back in Kwo?" asked Deel.

Uriah nodded. "I bought the faith she would return with me to Hope. I bought God's offerings and gave thanks, yet she refused to come." Uriah let out a deep sigh of resignation before mumbling, "I understand now why people are afraid to give up the thoughts of EGO. The pain may be uncomfortable, but it is a familiar one. I don't care if I ever go back to Hope again."

Deel said nothing for several moments. A wry smile crept across lips. "You sound like me."

"How's that?"

"Before I left Hope, I began to grow impatient with God. I had faith and gave thanks, just as you had, and

I too wanted His promises to manifest immediately. When they did not, I thought perhaps it was because God had something else in store for me, something even grander. But then I began to believe God had His own timeline. And He and I were not working on the same clock, so to speak. I grew more and more frustrated and impatient with Him. I began to believe that maybe I didn't deserve His promises, that perhaps I wasn't worthy."

"And now?" asked Uriah.

"Now I have come to believe His offerings always manifest immediately, but we must be willing to see them. We are the ones who hesitate and we are the ones who must become clear. When we buy the thoughts of the Source and pay the asking price—He delivers. I believe though, that sometimes our eyes are closed to His deliveries."

"How do you mean?"

"Take your grandfather for instance. For a long time I have been unhappy and wanted to return to Hope, but I was unwilling to take action, until I met him. Long before meeting your grandfather, I no longer wished to live with the thoughts of EGO, yet my feet did not take me in that direction. Can I blame God for this? Hope did not move and I did not see that God had already provided for me what I asked. I asked and God answered, yet my eyes were closed to His providing." Deel paused a moment and then said, "People say they want things in this life, yet they take no action to achieve those things."

Uriah looked at him puzzled, "But you have yet to return to Hope. How has God provided that for you?"

"Because I learned," said Deel softly, as he pointed to his chest, "that Hope has always been in here. God had already given me everything I asked for and He placed it in here. I chose not to see it. I chose not to pay His asking price. Hope," continued Deel "is not somewhere we must fight to reach. It is inside each of us. God provides this. But we must be willing to see it for ourselves."

It was then that Uriah realized his new friend had unwittingly provided the answer to the riddle given him by Percy and Tru.

Uriah knew immediately that this was what Percy and Tru wanted him to discover for himself. They wanted him to learn that that God had already placed Hope in his heart. Uriah suspected that buying the thoughts of EGO is what keeps Hope hidden deep inside them.

"Why do we not see it then?" Uriah asked.

Deel shook his head, "Perhaps because most have forgotten God exists, or at least about the ideas and products of God. EGO was good at convincing people of that. People have lived without the thoughts of God for a long time. You must travel back several generations when people could openly buy His thoughts without persecution."

Deel looked up at a hawk circling well overhead; he closed his eyes and took in a deep breath of air through his nose. Uriah thought in that moment he looked exactly like his father, Tru.

"I have also discovered people always have a choice to buy thoughts from God or from EGO, and no man can tell another from whom to buy. EGO has been in control for a long time, but I believe ultimately man will find his way back to God. A few know His thoughts are available, but are too filled with fear to act on them."

"What can be done then?"

"Let people know the thoughts of God are available," Deel answered. "Your grandfather helped me realize this. Follow the God and the Hope in your heart. If everyone agreed to buy their thoughts from the Source, then EGO and all the worlds' problems would miraculously disappear. One man with hope can counter the negativity of thousands."

"Do you believe that?" Uriah asked still somewhat skeptical.

"With all my heart," answered Deel, matter of factly.

"But we cannot tell others how to think, right?"

"Correct. But we can make them aware," smiled Deel. "After that, the choice is theirs."

Suddenly the hawk darted furiously downward; it had spotted its prey. The two men watched as the bird halted its dive and began gliding parallel a foot or so from the ground. The outstretched talons then thrust forward and, as quickly as it had begun, the hunt was over. The hawk began its ascent, a freshly caught rodent in its grip. The meal was the hawk's reward for its action.

"Do you see that hawk?" asked Deel.

"Of course," nodded Uriah.

"The hawk can circle for many hours, even days before it eats, yet it never doubts that eventually it will be successful," Deel told him, "A hawk always believes in its own power. It waits patiently, but does not hesitate to act when it must. We could all learn to be more like the hawk."

"By eating mice?" Uriah joked.

Uriah understood this well. He had experienced the power of the Source from his short time in Hope and now also the creeping doubt of EGO of which Tru had warned him to be wary. His new friend had experienced both on a much grander scale than he.

But Uriah continued to feel betrayal over the loss of both his grandfather and Akuna, and he struggled to reach that place of faith. Deel sensed his confusion.

"Ask to purchase the thoughts of clarity from God," advised Deel. "Far too many die miserably from the thoughts of EGO. It is up to you to see that your grandfather's death was not in vain."

Uriah gave him an obligatory nod, yet he was truly thankful for the wisdom of his new friend.

The two men set up camp for the evening. They decided to use the shrubs and hilly terrain as camouflage while they slept. It was a habit each had developed from their time in the wild. As they lay on their backs peering up at the stars, Uriah asked, "Are you afraid?"

"Afraid of what?"

"You bought the thoughts of God once and somehow EGO pulled you back to their product of damaging thoughts. Are you afraid the thoughts of EGO will return for you again?"

Deel shook his head slightly and chuckled, "No. I *know* EGO will return. I must choose not to buy the fear."

"Yes, you'll be fine as long as you feed the good wolf," said Uriah, attempting to impress his new friend. The moment the words left his mouth Uriah realized it was a story Deel probably knew well. The two men then looked at each other, and without another word, they both began laughing. It was obvious to them both they had been tutored by Tru, years apart.

As their laughter settled down, both men went silent and Uriah lay still looking up at the sky. It was filled with so many stars; there was hardly a spot he could look without seeing their illumination. It was in this moment; he decided he would return to Hope with Deel. That evening beneath the stars Uriah bought clarity and forgiveness from God and then peacefully drifted into a deep slumber.

Early the next morning, both men were awakened abruptly by the sound of footsteps nearby. They believed the wilderness was full of predators, but the deliberateness of the steps left no doubt they were human.

The two leapt from their bedrolls, scanning the area. About twenty feet from them a tall, haggard looking man cautiously approached. A scrawny, tired looking woman trailed a few steps behind him. Uriah sensed something familiar about them, but could not determine precisely what.

"Hello," said the man weakly. Uriah sensed they were obviously too hungry and tired to be afraid of strangers.

"Good morning," responded Deel cautiously, while Uriah nodded hello. For a moment both parties sized one another up. The four stood in a kind of face off, each eyeing the other two with suspicion. Finally Uriah broke his ranks beside Deel and extended his hand toward the man. "Hello, my name is Uriah. This is my friend Deel."

"Hello," repeated the man, taking Uriah's hand in his. "My name is Baran and this is my wife Yetta."

"Where are you from?" asked Uriah.

"We are from a town called Kwo. We have walked for many days and we are starving and exhausted."

Baran told them an old man had spoken to them about a place where the thoughts of God were available. He told them, if they wanted a life of possibilities, happiness, and love, they should leave Kwo and follow the stars to this place. It was then that Uriah recognized the man. He had seen him in Kwo many times, but the two had never spoken. Grandfather must have been busy, thought Uriah. If only he had followed his own words sooner.

Baran said they would often see the old man, and he would always nod a polite hello until, "One day he suddenly began to speak to us of this place by the sea," said Yetta softly. "We were afraid, but his words...," she gasped with tears forming in her eyes, "his words were honest and full of passion."

"Welcome," said Deel inviting them to sit. "You must be hungry?"

Baran nodded, smiling gratefully. "We have walked many miles without food and water and very little sleep. This journey has made us old in a very short time." The four sat down in the makeshift camp, each took a deep sigh of relief. Uriah and Deel laid out their remaining food and water and began preparing something resembling a breakfast. The four of them ate while they talked.

"My wife and I thought about the old man's words," Baran began. "They sparked something within us." Deel looked to Uriah, expecting him to ask their new guests about his grandfather, but instead Uriah remained silent.

"We had been so filled with doubt and fear. It was all we knew," cried Yetta. "His stories were so powerful," she continued between mouthfuls of bread. "We took it as a sign that if a man would risk his life to speak to us on the thoughts of God, it must be true."

"His words tugged at our hearts," said Baran reaffirming Yetta's words. "We feared the Company would harm us, but something within us said his words were true. He said it was a place we could live freely with the thoughts of God. Our daughter died one year ago, and we were alone. We decided to take a chance."

Uriah smiled broadly. He felt a warm glow of satisfaction wash over him. Perhaps his grandfather would live on after all; certainly his words were having a profound effect on others.

The group would rest in this spot together, but they knew they could not afford to stay in one place long. Their food supply was nearly gone, and they would have to stop in the next town for supplies. Baran and Yetta were eager to travel with them. They all agreed they could reach the next village by afternoon.

In the next town they visited, Deel and Uriah would share stories of Hope with the local townspeople. Uriah would continue the message of his grandfather, sharing with others' about the thoughts of God. He was cautious yet determined to keep his grandfather's legacy alive.

"The more people who know of Hope," said Uriah to the others, "the less power EGO has. The more people who buy the thoughts of God, the less pain and misery EGO has to sell."

"Look who is coming around now?" smiled Deel jokingly. Deel may have been having fun with him, but he was right, Uriah was inspired and growing more determined by the moment.

"You have a sense of humor like your father," Uriah joked back and the two men laughed again.

Although the four were only able to manifest enough food for one meal each, they secretly spoke about the products of the Source with the locals. They were risking arrest with each passing moment; yet planting the seeds of God right beneath the nose of EGO. Uriah and Deel encouraged other townspeople to share with their neighbors whenever possible. Many refused, but a few hesitantly agreed. They didn't see it yet, but a movement and a shift in consciousness was taking form.

"They are growing tired of the misery," said Deel. "They are learning it is time to rise up against EGO and make a choice, a choice as to where to buy their thoughts."

"Percy told me that humanity once had a choice from whom to purchase thoughts. Most choose EGO," said Uriah.

"And my father once said we must be careful not to take the thoughts of God for granted. Believe me I know," said Deel.

The next morning, the four were joined by two more people fleeing towns owned by EGO. The following day, three more people had joined the group in their exodus from the thoughts of EGO. Word of the Source, although spoken only in whispers to a select few, was beginning to spread.

These new refugees brought with them frightening news of EGO. They had heard rumors of men spreading the word of the Source in various towns and EGO meant to capture them. The group, although free, were careful to stay a step ahead of the authorities at all times.

"We're going to need more food to feed our growing population," joked Baran.

"We are far from a town," said Uriah. "We will have to buy faith that we will be fed."

He thought of a story he had read in one of the books Percy had given him. It was called the Holy Bible. All books, especially those involving faith of any kind were outlawed in Kwo. Uriah was fascinated with stories of faith and the power of manifestation. He read about a man named Jesus and His followers. Uriah consumed His message of hope and salvation.

His favorite story involving Jesus was how Jesus fed thousands of people who had come to hear him speak. He did this simply by having an overwhelming faith that God would provide enough food for all. Miraculously, enough fish and bread appeared to feed the entire crowd, which was estimated at five thousand. Uriah remembered a passage in the book where Jesus claimed that all people could do as he did, through God. Uriah prayed asking for the faith that the rapidly growing group would be fed. Within moments of his prayers they were joined by several more people fleeing the towns of the Company. With them they brought supplies of food and water, enough for all. Uriah's faith grew. Having witnessed this miracle of faith, he vowed to never buy the doubt of EGO again.

Each day, their numbers grew. Men and woman, several with children, straggled in from unmarked towns along the vast wasteland. Towns the group had recently passed through. These new comers were encouraged to follow the stars toward the sea. Most walked night and day to escape the thoughts of the Company, all with little or no food. All who came, had made a choice to act on the words of Deel and Uriah, and journey to this magical place called Hope.

One day a young woman entered the camp. Uriah thought he recognized her from his travels. She walked directly to him and took his hand. She placed something in his palm and curled his fingers closed into a fist.

"Months ago, you gave me this for a piece of stale bread. You tried to offer me something greater by telling me about a place where the thoughts of God were available, but I was unable to receive your message, until now. I wanted to return this. It belongs to you."

Uriah opened his hand and in his palm was the beautiful Larimar stone he had traded months earlier. "The stone made me realize," continued the woman, "there are still things of beauty in this world, if we are willing to look for them. That is why I am here."

The nights at camp were filled with questions. Those new to the group were anxious to hear tales of Hope and the thoughts offered by the Source. Is it possible to have dreams? Can anyone buy thoughts from the Source? Can we openly express love? All were anxious to experience life outside of Company rule.

In the day, the group moved swiftly, conscious to stay ahead of the authorities. A few days later, they reached another town. It was the last one remaining before Hope. Their numbers now equaled forty.

"There are far too many of us to go into this town," said Deel. "We have enough food to make it to Hope; it is too risky to go in. We should pass by this one."

Uriah protested. "I made a promise to a man here," he said. "The girl's name is Natta and I promised her grandfather I would come for her. I told this man I would tell his granddaughter of Hope." While the others waited outside the city, Uriah entered alone. When he emerged less than an hour later, Natta and her grandfather were by his side.

Four days later, the group approached the entrance to Hope. Tru was there to greet them, just as he had been when Uriah first arrived months earlier.

"I see ya' made it back," said Tru. "And ya' brought some friends with ya'."

"Yes," smiled Uriah. "My friend and I told them about the thoughts of God. We were hoping there might be a place for them here. They need to be cleaned and fed, and we told them we could find them a place to stay. That is of course after they meet the old man," Uriah said with a grin.

"We?" asked Tru. "Who is yer friend?"

"I am," said Deel stepping out from the rear of the group to reveal himself. Tru's eyes locked on his son. His mouth hung open in amazement and joy. Tears began to form in the large mans eyes.

Tru and his son stood staring at one another in silence. Finally they embraced, neither had yet to speak a word, then both men began to sob uncontrollably.

"Come," said Uriah to the group. "Let's leave them alone so they may get reacquainted."

Then Uriah led the group past the sign on the trail toward a place called Hope.

□■ FIFTEEN ■□

The new residents to Hope had settled in nicely to their surroundings. Things were as Deel and Uriah had told them. Products of the Source were available for purchase without fear of retribution, and each individual began to carve out the destiny of their choice by freely purchasing the thoughts of God.

They bought intuition and compassion. Each was allowed to express love and share the dreams and ideas of God for the first time in their lives. After many years of suppression, they would need practice to access more offerings of the Source. Although these new citizens of Hope were no longer forced to purchase the thoughts of EGO, they needed both patience and persistence in order to best utilize these thoughts. They were encouraged to purchase faith, as a replacement to the fear they had owned for many years; they were taught to practice meditation, as a means of listening to the voice of God and prayer as a vessel for asking.

Many struggled and became ill as a result of the internal strife going on within them. Even from a distance, EGO fought to enslave them and this manifested in some slight physical degeneration. They were encouraged to push through their resistance and continue to purchase the thoughts of the Source. In a very short time, all would learn to clearly understand and act on the voice of God. And soon after, they were easily able to manifest His thoughts on their own and call upon His guidance, when needed.

As for Tru, if there was any separation between him and his son, it had quickly faded. The two men appeared not to miss a step. Their first days together were spent in gratitude and appreciation for their long-awaited reunion. Deel told Tru stories of his time outside of Hope. He told of the terrible conditions he encountered and how he had become caught up in the cycle of disempowering thoughts. Breaking away from the products of EGO was no small feat, for Deel had endured much pain and hardship, yet the responsibility was his and his alone. He vowed to his father and most importantly, to himself, to continuously work on feeding the good wolf.

Tru passed no judgment on his son, choosing to buy only gratitude for his return. His son had returned safely, and that was all he asked of God. When EGO had attempted to sell Tru doubt and worry surrounding his son, he refused to purchase such notions. During Deel's absence, he had bought an unwavering belief his son would return. To Tru, his son's return was a foregone conclusion, and he also blessed the day Uriah arrived in Hope.

"I wanna' thank ya' fer bringin' ma' boy back," he told Uriah.

"Actually, it was he who brought me back," Uriah said humbly.

Either way, noted Tru, his son was back and for this he was grateful.

"Ne'er any doubt in ma' mind he'd return," Tru said with a chuckle.

For Uriah, more patience and prayer was required. For now, spreading the word of Hope and the thoughts of the Source was where Uriah put his focus. "They'll be more people coming to Hope," he told Percy.

He was right, at least initially. The first week after his return saw seven more refugees from neighboring towns filter in. All had come to escape the thoughts of EGO, but more importantly, to fulfill their glory with the products of God.

After the first week, just one more soul straggled across the threshold of Hope. The exodus from the towns of EGO seemed to come to a halt, as quickly as it began. Uriah and Deel had spoken to many about the Source but without consistent reinforcement, the people in the neighboring towns quickly fell back under the grip of EGO. The thought police had reinforced their hold on the existing customer base. Hope was hardly in danger of overpopulating. The unwillingness to leave their present situations and the fear of the journey to Hope continued to hold most of the EGO-held population locked in their present lives of misery and sadness.

Uriah knew in his heart he must continue to carry the message to others. He would tell anyone who would listen about the thoughts of God and their availability to all. Hope had been designed as a sanctuary for the thoughts of God, free from the evil of EGO. It was a place where one could fulfill his or her destiny and live as God intended. All that was required was to accept God's offering and pay the asking price. Hope offered freedom from the confusion where conflicting thoughts were not given momentum.

Minds were free to grow without weeds. But Uriah understood, should he continue to carry the message, eventually the town of Hope would not hold all the people. He had to convince them Hope was in their hearts and minds just as he had discovered. He would tell them Hope was not a place they were forced to reach in order to access the thoughts of God.

"I must continue my grandfather's message," said Uriah to Percy. "They must be told that the thoughts of God are not restricted by a geographical location on a map. They must learn that Hope and the offerings of the Source are already in their hearts, if only they trust in its power. Besides," Uriah said softly, "I believe God has no one left but us to keep His message alive."

Percy was careful to remind Uriah of how cunning and patient the power of EGO can be. Although he knew Uriah was familiar with EGO, Percy stressed his need to stay in faith and pray often.

"EGO knows you are coming this time," warned Percy. "They will fight with everything they have, to keep their customers and save their business. In order to maintain control of the minds of the people, they will kill you as an example to others."

In spite of these dangers which lie ahead, Uriah prepared to spread the message of the Source. Many of the new people who had recently arrived in Hope volunteered to accompany him, but it was a journey he insisted on taking alone.

"Where will ya' go?" asked Tru.

"Wherever the thoughts of the Source take me first," answered Uriah. "The prisoners of EGO are everywhere, and there is nowhere my grandfather's message and the products of the Source are not needed."

"Are ya' sure this is what ya' wanna' do? It's right dangerous out there in the world a' thoughts."

"I do," answered Uriah. "My grandfather made me realize that one man 'can' make a difference, if he believes. That even one man is capable of great things, if only he truly believes it to be so. And a great man once told me that, if the thoughts of God are alive, there will always be Hope," he said winking at Tru. The two men then embraced.

"Looks like yer teachin' me now," Tru smiled.

Uriah bid farewell to Tru and Deel, grateful they had been reunited. He packed his Bible given to him by Percy and bought a generous portion of faith and love. "It is something I must do to honor my grandfather," he told them.

"When will you return?" asked Percy.

"When I feel called to. After I have spread the word of the Source," answered Uriah.

"You may not get the message to everyone," warned Percy. "There will always be those who EGO will continue to control."

"Perhaps," smiled Uriah. "But I must try. I must plant as many Godly seeds of thought as possible. Look at the impact of my grandfather's words. Dozens of people have now been lifted from lives of misery and despair because of his message of God."

Uriah knew the process would be long and dangerous, but he had faith in God's products and a passion to carry the message to all. He also believed there were many who would come to know Hope, if only they were made aware. He said goodbye to Percy and left them to continue to spread the word of God.

Within several weeks of Uriah's departure, reports began to trickle into the gates of Hope. Many towns in the region near them were beginning to change. Slowly at first. But soon people across the region were refusing to buy the thoughts of EGO, too many in fact for EGO to capture and imprison. They were taking back their communities and their minds. Word quickly spread like a wildfire blazing out of control. Uriah's message grew exponentially, and words of the Source sprung up in towns hundreds of miles away, towns which Uriah never entered.

Within a short time, the products of the Source were as ubiquitous as the air they breathed. The thought-police of EGO was unable to keep up with the growing stream of offenders purchasing the thoughts of God. Attempts at arrest by the police were futile. And soon after, EGO was run out of the towns, first one village then the next, and on it continued. The thoughts of the Source were rapidly becoming known to everyone, and it was obvious to the people they could access these thoughts where and when they chose. The message of the Source was being carried on its own. And Uriah's mission had taken on a life of its own. In his heart, he felt the tug to return to Hope, after months away. He faced in the direction of the sea and followed the brightest star toward Hope. In less than a week, he would be home.

"I will continue to carry your words, grandfather," he whispered. In his heart, he continued to buy the faith that Akuna would one day come to Hope. He had bought a miracle, and he knew that with God all things were possible.

At that very moment, miles away from Uriah, an attractive young girl approached the gates of Hope. She was weak and worn, and it was obvious she had traveled a great distance. The girl had a small crescent shaped birthmark on her neck.

It was Tru who met her first, "Hello, my name is Tru." he said warmly. "Welcome to a place called Hope."

"Hello. My name is Akuna," she smiled.

◻▪ BUYER'S WARRANTY ▪◻

In the beginning of this story, I told you that I bought this idea from God. This was true. What I didn't tell you is how well acquainted I am with His competition. In fact, I've been buying from "them" for years. The goal of the competition has and always will be to replace the merchandise of God and steal His clientele.

Their product may be packaged in a thousand different ways, but it's always the same no matter the name, just plain old dung. And we buy it up by the truckload. Their salesmen follow up behind God with delicious counteroffers to the Source. Offers they know we can't seem to live without. They sell us, "can't do it's," the "I'm not good enough's," the "I don't have the time or money" and the "That'll never work," until it's spilling out of our ears. The competition is a very successful company. I should know, I've been a platinum customer for a long time.

When we buy from the competition, we may not even be aware we are buying the lies, yet most of us cling to their merchandise, like a crossbar on a roller coaster. Their tactics are subtle and unassuming, assuring us that their brand of product benefits us in some way, and we buy it all on credit.

As I mentioned, I am familiar with the product line of God's competition, painfully so, in fact. For years, I have chosen to delay the grace of God's heavenly offerings. I have been putting items offered by the Source on layaway. I have shelved countless ideas and inspirations offered me by the Source, items left to gather dust in the storage unit of my mind. I've piled decades of products one atop the other, the trip to the Greek isles lay dormant and sandwiched somewhere between writing the great American novel and opening an animal rescue shelter. These offerings from God, and more, are stored somewhere in the back of my mind with the invoice still stamped payment due.

The thing is, I have grown tired of the goods of God's competition, and that is why I bought this idea from God and willingly paid His price. If any of the merchandise from God's competition sounds familiar to you, it's probably because you and I have been shopping at the same store. If this is the case, then please don't fret.

I understand God has an excellent return policy, whether you bought it from Him or not!

□■ AUTHOR'S NOTE ■□

I began writing *A Place Called Hope* in September of 2013. The collaborative effort of writing, editing, printing and publishing a book can be a stressful, time-consuming endeavor, to say the least.

By February of 2014, with the book nearing completion, I had reached my breaking point. The months of writing in a vacuum, correcting, reshaping and restructuring the text had taken an enormous toll on my psyche. I was physically, mentally, emotionally and yes, ironically enough, even spiritually exhausted. I had become too much involved in my "self" and desperately needed to break out of the life-draining cycle I had created. Much like Uriah, I had become filled with doubt and insecurity in my heart and mind. So, one day I asked God for a sign or message that I was indeed on the right path. I chose to buy my thoughts from Him rather than from His competition. Now, I have always believed that the best way to "get out" of your own head is to get into service of another and as fate would have it, that same day I received an email from a volunteer organization in desperate need of help. I thought this could be the sign I was seeking…so I responded.

Within a few days, I had begun volunteering at a local rescue mission a few nights a week, caring for underprivileged children while their parents attended developmental and job skills training classes. For two hours a night, three nights a week, I am now at the mercy of these beautiful, energetic and wildly entertaining miniature humans. To them, I am but an oversized toy for them to bend, climb, ride, shape and manipulate as they see fit, and I love every minute of it. Within a very short time, they have managed to capture my heart and also help me burn off a few unwanted pounds. I had asked God with faith, gave thanks, and took action…and He provided.

To me, working with these children has been an absolute gift. It was my intention to be of service to others, yet what I have been given in return has been infinitely more rewarding. I thank God each day for allowing me the opportunity to work with these amazing kids. Is this a miracle? Perhaps, perhaps not. I suppose it depends on your definition. In my mind, there is no question it is. You see, it wasn't only about the incredible change in my heart and attitude, but in the physical, tangible signs I received along the way. I learned that God can be quite literal in His answers. I asked God for a sign that I was on the right path with *A Place Called Hope* and He obliged, literally.

You see, my first day arriving at the mission, I was advised to make a right turn on to Hope Drive, my first sign from God. As I turned in to the parking lot, a large concrete sign told me I had reached my destination. It read, "Welcome to the Village of Hope," a definite second sign. I had no prior knowledge of this sign or the mission before writing *A Place Called Hope*. Yet here was a clear sign marking my way and letting me know I was in fact on the right path. Once inside the children's center, the word Hope appeared in no less than half a dozen places. Painted road signs, marquees, and a wall mural of a farm with a water tower, each with the word Hope painted on them. These messages were a clear indication that God had intended a path for me to follow, with His signposts marking the way. Through buying God's thoughts and taking action with the mission, I was able to see His message. I knew immediately I was on the right path. Each individual sign of Hope was a miracle by itself, collectively they were too much to ignore.

I have learned that in our darkest moments, when we may feel God is ignoring us, He is merely waiting for us to ask for His help, or more likely, waiting for payment on his offer: a payment of thanks, gratitude and action. So, when you find yourself in those dark times in your life, and you most certainly will (thank God for that), listen to the thoughts of God and pay His fee. Then look for your own personal signs of Hope.

To purchase additional copies of *A Place Called Hope* or share your experiences and stories about the thoughts of God with other readers, please visit our website at:

www.APlaceCalledHopeBook.com or visit
www.JamesJohnRoss.com

Chat with the Author

Let us know what you Think

Leave a Review

Share your personal experiences of living with the thoughts of God.

If you would like the author to speak to your organization or charity, please email *James.Ross@pacbell.net* or visit
www.JamesJohnRoss.com

Raise Awareness About the Power of Thought and Create Global Change!

Help spread the uplifting message of *A Place Called Hope*, and encourage others to purchase the thoughts of God, by sharing copies of this book with family, friends and co workers. Please communicate about this book on social media, blog posts and websites. Also, feel free to post a review on Amazon, and please post the link to our website. We would like to thank you all for helping to raise world consciousness by spreading this message about the thoughts of God. They are available to us all!